YOU'RE BROOM OR MINE?

MAGIC AND MAYHEM BOOK 8

ROBYN PETERMAN

VISIT MY WEBSITE

BOOKS IN THIS SERIES

HIT HERE FOR THE WEBSITE PAGE WITH ALL THE BOOKS!

ACKNOWLEDGMENTS

I adore the Magic and Mayhem Series. It started on a dare and I see no end in sight. Expanding the town of Assjacket makes me happy. In the beginning, I had no clue Zelda had a twin, but I couldn't be more delighted that she does. Zach kicks some major butt and my dryad, Willow, was so much fun to write. I even created a new language in this one. Puntreelish. Much to my family's horror, I'm still speaking Puntreelish even though I'm done writing the book. LOL

As always, while writing is a solitary experience getting a book into the world is a group project.

Renee — Thank you for all your support, your friendship, your deviously brilliant mind and for being the best Cookie ever. You saved my butt on this one. Forever in your debt.

Wanda — Thank you for knowing what I mean even when I don't. LOL You are the best and this writing business wouldn't be any fun without you. You make the journey more fun.

Sara — Thank you for saving me from scary grammar mistakes. You rock. And thank you for letting me be late. LOL

Heather, Susan and Wanda — Thank you for being kickass betas. You are all wonderful.

Rebecca — Thank you. As always, your cover captured what was in my mind perfectly.

Steve, Henry and Audrey — Thank you. The three of you are my world. Without you, none of this would make sense. I love you.

DEDICATION

For Heather, my new buddy with the eagle eyes!

BOOK DESCRIPTION

YOUR BROOM OR MINE?

**What's a Tree Sprite to do when she's stumped?
Get to the root of the problem, of course.**

Only I *wood* get stuck in a tree with the Warlock I love
camped out next to it mea-culpa-ing for being a turdwaffle
for the last decade.

What should I do about it?

Umm... stay in the tree and enjoy the show.

Location: Assjacket, West Virginia (Who in their right mind
named this town?)

Mission: Get out of the tree and dropkick the Warlock
who forgot to mention he was in love with me until I was
stuck in a tree.

Obstacles: Just about everything... crazy foul mouthed
witches, accident-prone shifters and a musical production
of *Jaws.*

The Problem: A vicious Slug shifter who will do anything to ruin my future.

The Solution: With a little luck, a whole bunch of salt, a pinch of magic and the help of my certifiable new buddies, I might just survive long enough to put down some new roots.

And if the journey in the woods gets too crazy? Not a problem. I'll just branch out and take the psycho-path.

CHAPTER ONE

My stomach flipped. Then my stomach flopped.

It wasn't just my stomach. It was my brain, my emotions and my magic. I was a hot mess and a possible arboreal disaster waiting to happen.

While I was tempted to yell *timber*, I wasn't exactly falling, and I didn't want to alarm the boys. They'd been so protective and kind. Not to mention, I wasn't technically a tree.

With each passing day, it was getting more obvious that my body had healed from its near-death state and it was time to *leaf*, but I choked every time I tried to force the words from my lips.

And oh, my Goddess... *the puns*. I was speaking the language of my people. It wasn't surprising, due to my *leafly*, umm... lovely surroundings, but I'd given Puntreelish up about ninety years ago when I was five—not that I looked ninety-five, thank the Goddess. Most dryads stopped aging around thirty give or take a few life rings... Crap. Years—give or take a few years.

Should I stay or should I go? The Clash wasn't going to be able to help me with this one. Decisions were harsh. I hadn't made one in what felt like ages, and it had been freaking fantastic.

Should I open my eyes or keep floating in the sparkling rainbow kaleidoscope? My stomach tingled with the sensation of riding a lightning-fast roller coaster. Magic was exquisite, delicate and ethereal. Simply staying still enabled my mind to travel to otherworldly places—safe places.

It also enabled me to avoid reality. Definitely not my normal MO. But *reality* was unknown and not very promising at the moment.

Done. The answer was to stay. I'd keep my eyes closed and defy gravity. Elphaba knew what she was talking about. Witches—even wicked ones—were delightful.

"Wakey, wakey, little dryad," the huge oak whispered in a melodic tone. *"Time to spruce up for the day ahead."*

I smiled and groaned. Trees were very punny.

Normally, being inside a tree was peaceful. It was second nature to my kind. However, being stuck inside of a tree for a month after nearly dying was a little a-tree-o-phying. Of course, the almost dying part wasn't all that pleasant, either —more like a bloody vicious battle that visited me nightly in my dreams. The voodoo witch, Henrietta Smith, who went by Marie Laveau, had tried to destroy me with the darkest magic I'd ever come across. She'd almost succeeded. However, that was the past, and I was trying my best to *leaf* it there.

"*Leaf me alone, Sponge Bob,*" I said with an exaggerated yawn. "*Need my beauty sleep.*"

The huge tree chuckled. The vibration felt like a small tremor from an earthquake. It tickled all over and made me sigh with content.

"*Sleep is not required for your beauty, little one. You are one of the most exquisite creatures on the Goddess's green earth. However, your leaf of absence is coming to an end quite soon,*" Sponge Bob said.

Like I said… punny.

And while I was all for a good tree pun or joke since I was a dryad, a month *was* a seriously long time to only be able to chat with gargantuan wooden oaks. Not that I was ungrateful. I wasn't. I adored the trees. Plus, Sponge Bob and the boys had saved my life. Not only had they healed me, they'd rocked me back to sleep after every single nightmare. Repayment would be impossible, but I'd figure out something.

"*So, it's time for me to make like a tree and leaf.*" A pit of despair formed in my stomach.

Sponge Bob's warm spring-scented magic surrounded me and cuddled me like a baby. "*Little Willow, you can't hide forever. Your body is healed. It's your spirit that needs help right now. There are many who mourn you. You leaf quite an impression on people.*"

I was tempted to ask who mourned me, but I bit the words back. I had no clue if the warlock I pined for was alive or if Henrietta Smith had ended Zach like she'd tried to end me. And then there was also Zorro, my best friend who might have perished as well in the battle. Henrietta had

3

collected rare magical creatures so she could drink their blood and harness their power. Zach had been the product of a powerful witch and warlock. It had made him particularly delectable to the evil crone. Zorro, a fainting goat Shifter, was basically a unicorn in the Shifter world. He was able to wield magic almost as well as any warlock, which made him a treasured find for the maniacal bitch. Zorro also fainted under pressure, which made him an easy target. Oh, Goddess, Zorro. I had a vague memory of him alive, and I held onto it for all I was worth. But Zach? I didn't know what had happened to him and that figured prominently into my night terrors. Again, far easier to avoid physical existence and just live it up for the rest of my days in a tree.

"*Soon,*" I whispered.

Sponge Bob hugged me tighter. "*As you wish, little one.*"

"*I have a pleasan-tree to share,*" Grumpy announced.

"*How pleasant?*" Doc inquired suspiciously.

Not only had Sponge Bob sheltered me, his buddies had also aided in my healing. The five trees had taken me in without question and lovingly absorbed my barely alive body into their own massive wooden ones. Sponge Bob was the tree who had kept me cradled safely within. Sleepy, Doc, Sneezy and Grumpy had attached their branches to Sponge Bob to provide him with more magic. They were basically now one big-assed tree with five trunks.

For them to join together like this was unheard of and beautiful beyond imagination.

Grumpy cleared his throat and pondered aloud as he was wont to do. "*I'm undeciduous about how pleasant my pleasan-tree is. It might be an oversimp-leaf-ication to say pleasant."*

"Does this pleasan-tree include potty words?" Sneezy asked. *"Remember, we do have a guest."*

"Umm, guys," I said with a laugh. *"I'm cool with potty words. I use them. Often."*

"And you use them quite well," Sponge Bob congratulated me. *"However, I do have to concede that our witchy leader, Zelda of the Poopy Crap Mouth, has a way with the potty language that verges on poe-tree. She has a mouth like an illus-tree-ous sailor on a life-long bender. Very impressive."*

I grinned. It was an understatement. Zelda's use of curse words was positively inspired. *Zelda of the Poopy Crap Mouth* was yet one more magnificent person to whom I owed my life. The trees were her minions, and she had brought me to them. She was also the twin sister of the warlock I loved and who I feared was dead.

So, I avoided thinking about him. It hurt a lot less than dealing with the truth.

"I'd like to hear your pleasan-tree, Grumpy," I told my friend, buying more time.

"I'd be ex-tree-mely excited to share. What does a Christmas tree and a priest have in common?" Grumpy asked.

"I'm stumped," Doc replied.

"Anyone?" Grumpy called out.

"Nope," Sneezy said.

"No clue," Sleepy said.

"Willow? Would you like to guess?" Grumpy asked cheerfully. He really was the complete antithesis of his name.

"Umm... no," I said with a giggle. I was certain the answer

5

would be fabulously *knotty*. While Grumpy wasn't a grump at all, his pleasan-trees were slightly *out-tree-geous* for an oak.

"Their balls are just for decoration!" Grumpy shouted then burst into high-pitched squeaky laughter as the ground shook beneath us.

"Grumpy, that was quite shady and disgusting," Sponge Bob admonished. *"However, I can top it."*

"Tree-mendous," Grumpy said, still chuckling. *"Go for it."*

"What did the wind say to the palm tree?" Sponge Bob asked.

"Stumped again," Doc said.

"Hold onto your nuts, this is no ordinary blow job," Sponge Bob choked out as his entire root system jiggled.

I laughed right along with him. Sponge Bob had been such a gracious host. He and the four others had fussed over me and made me feel welcome the entire time I'd been their guest. I couldn't have asked for a better arboreal home. But even I knew my time with the boys was coming to an end.

"Very punny—both of you," I said as lime-green pops of glitter burst around my head-wreath. Inside the tree, my body was a blur of golden and bright green sparkles. Gravity had no hold on me in this state. I vibrated and shifted colors with the heartbeats of the trees. *"I've got one. How do you know when a tree has had too much to drink?"*

The boys were silent, but I could feel them rumble and snicker in anticipation.

"It won't stop trunk-texting its ax," I said, bracing myself so I didn't get sucked up into a branch by accident. Occasion-

6

ally, when the boys got giggly, I got tossed around. Trunks were far more comfortable than branches.

All five enormous oaks shrieked with laugher. The sound warmed my heart and calmed my soul. Ironically, for their size, you'd think that trees would have deep grumbling laughs. Nope, when trees laughed it sounded as if they'd swallowed a vat of helium. It was every kind of fabulous.

Although I couldn't see a thing, I could hear the sound of their leaves shudder and hiss with delight. I knew if I opened my eyes and let my mind wander, I would discover what was happening outside the safety of Sponge Bob's trunk, but I hadn't felt exactly brave.

I'd never thought of myself as a coward. However, I worried that if I went back out into the world it would be more devastating than dying.

"*I have another,*" I said, needing their laughter. It was the best medicine. "*Why couldn't the evergreen land a date?*"

"*I guaran-tree I do not know the answer,*" Sleepy announced grandly.

"*That was sappy,*" Sneezy pointed out.

"*Take it or leaf it,*" Sleepy said with a giggle. "*Tell us the answer, lovely little Willow!*"

I grinned. "*It was so busy pining after an unavailable tree that it never really branched out.*"

No one laughed.

My grin disappeared.

I'd hit a little too close to home with that one—my home. Crap. I'd pined for a man who didn't think of me as more than a friend… and I'd never branched out to find someone who might love me back.

That was pathetic.

I was pathetic.

"What is it that you fear, Willow?" Sponge Bob asked kindly.

I hadn't put words to my thoughts yet. Speaking my fears would make them real. Was I being ridiculous? Yes. Would my mother—Goddess rest her beautiful soul—have a fit that I'd lost my balls somewhere along the way? Absolutely. Would my handsome and brave father who'd perished along with my mother fifty years ago tell me to pull up my big girl panties and live my life to the fullest and *bushiest?* You bet. Were dryads known as wimps in the magical world? No.

Did a man define me?

Even the hottest warlock alive?

No. No. No. My *forestration* level was at an all-time high.

"My balls," I said.

"I'm sorry, what?" Sponge Bob asked, clearly confused.

"As in tes-tree-cles?" Doc asked, perplexed.

"Umm... kind of," I said with a laugh. *"My metaphorical balls. I've lost them."*

Sleepy swayed in concentration. *"While trees do have nuts, it's a different kind of nut you're referring to. Correct?"*

"Correct," I told him with a grin. I was going to miss these boys when I left.

Grumpy cleared his throat. *"Speaking of metaphorical cojones, would any of you ever go on the acorn diet?"*

"Does this pertain to the conversation?" Sponge Bob asked with a sigh.

"*Not at all,*" Grumpy said. "*I just thought I'd add a little levity to the hairy sac chat.*"

"*I'd like to answer the query,*" Sneezy volunteered.

"*Fine,*" Sponge Bob said. "*And then no more jokes. We must discuss where Willow lost her nards.*"

I was tempted to stop them, but I wanted to know the answer.

"*I would never go on the acorn diet,*" Sneezy said. "*It's NUTS!*"

All five trees trembled with laughter. The jokes were just awful, but the company was perfect.

"*Pipe down,*" Sponge Bob told his buddies. "*Although, I must say that was a good one, Grumpy. But back to our little dryad's missing knotty bits... The only way to find your absen-tree jewels is to go back out into the world and search for them.*"

The wise oak made an excellent point. I needed more advice. Following my own hadn't gone too well.

"*What would you think of a girl who'd loved a man who didn't love her in return for an entire decade?*" I asked, laying it all out.

"*He's nuts and not the metaphorical kind,*" Grumpy grumbled.

"*No. Maybe I'm nuts,*" I said. "*Maybe I should just let it go and move on.*"

"*Is that what you want, little dryad?*" Sleepy asked.

"*Nope. But Mick Jagger says you can't always get what you want.*"

"*Does this Mick Jagger have balls?*" Sponge Bob inquired.

I laughed. "*Yes, and very tight spandex pants. He's a Rolling Stone. Maybe I'll take a page out of his book.*"

Doc tsked. *"Oh Willow, no, no, no. A rolling stone never settles in one place for long. You will never gather moss... or love or friends or a home... and spandex is so eighties."*

The thought was depressing—not the spandex part, that was accurate—but no more depressing than unrequited love. Dryads lived for many centuries. I'd bounced around many a forest in my time and there were more left to discover. A fresh start was what I needed. A rolling stone didn't sound too bad. But I needed a few clarifications about my current friends and love of my life before I started spinning through my new life.

"Boys, can I ask a question?"

"Absolu-tree," Sponge Bob replied.

"Is Zach alive or dead?"

The trees were silent and my stomach dropped to my toes.

"Open your eyes, Willow," Sponge Bob urged. *"Look and see for yourself. It's the first step in finding your hairy magic beans."*

I sighed and silently agreed. The mighty oak was correct. However, the variety of nicknames for balls was astounding.

"You're right. Can I come back and visit you some day?" I whispered, screwing up the courage to open my eyes and take a peek at the world I'd avoided for the past month.

"You always have a home in us. We have bonded and I am now your tree... a father of sorts," Sponge Bob said with pride. *"And as your wooden pappy, I must tell you if you truly want to locate your gonads, you must be brave and reenter the world beyond."*

"You're my tree now?" I asked with wonder. It was rare for

a dryad to bond with a tree. Contrary to popular belief, most of us went from tree to tree for centuries. To have a tree to call one's own was an honor beyond honors. My mom and dad would have been elated for me and would have approved of Sponge Bob heartily. An orphaned dryad finally had a home of her own.

"*Indeed, I am yours, child,*" Sponge Bob said. "*And I couldn't be more tree-lighted.*"

My smile was so wide it hurt my mouth. "*I couldn't be more tree-lighted either.*"

"*And by proxy, we are your uncles—or rela-tree-ives as I like to say,*" Grumpy added.

"*Yes, yes, yes,*" Doc said with a high-pitched squeal of joy. "*We've always wanted a little tree sprite of our own.*"

"*You're a tree-mendous gift to us,*" Sneezy said. "*We are gra-tree-fied with our new anses-tree. You are loved, little Willow.*"

"*I love all of you too,*" I whispered. The thought of having someplace that I truly belonged was magical.

"*Back to your mission,*" Sleepy reminded me. "*You must find your wrinkled prunes. We are rooting for you.*"

My arboreal family certainly had a way with words.

"*I can do this,*" I said, taking a deep breath.

"*We have faith in you, little one,*" Grumpy said. "*Faith that you will indeed find your meat clackers and wear them well.*"

"*Thank you,*" I said with a giggle. The intention was supportive. The wording was iffy. "*Balls. I want my balls back. And I'm going to Mick Jagger my way through life until I find them.*"

"*Remember when your stones get tired of rolling, you have a place with us to rest your weary head and change your spandex* pants," Sponge Bob said. "*We are your home now and can replenish your power with an embrace.*"

Grumpy rustled his leaves. "*You're our little tree-hugger now.*"

"*Thank you. You have no idea how much that means to me,*" I said, letting my magic open up and consume me.

"*On three,*" Doc said encouragingly. "*Open your eyes on three.*"

"*One,*" Sneezy said.

"*Two,*" Sleepy chimed in.

"*Three,*" I said, opening my eyes and gasping with joy. "*Oh thank Goddess, Zach's alive.*"

CHAPTER TWO

Zach wasn't dead. My heart raced with relief and happiness. He and Zelda were arguing next to Sponge Bob. They were mirror images of each other and beautiful.

Leaning in closer, but staying hidden in the Sponge Bob's trunk, I listened. Eavesdropping wasn't good form, but looking out at the world and reentering it were two entirely different things. Watching them was fascinating.

Zelda's wild red hair blew in the early afternoon breeze, and the sun framed the sister and brother in their stand-off. "You stink," she announced, slapping her hands on her hips and eyeing her brother with disgust.

While Zach looked exhausted and a little thinner, he also looked hopeful for the first time since I'd known him. He'd been sold at birth to the viciously evil, human voodoo witch, Henrietta Smith. She'd used his blood and magic to hang onto her youth and beauty. He'd been tied to her his entire life by an evil curse. But the haunted despair that had always lived in his eyes was gone. The curse had clearly been broken.

Swiping at a single tear that rolled down my cheek, I thanked the Goddess for sparing Zach and giving him a life that could be joyous. Zach, more than anyone I knew, deserved to be happy.

I had always hoped to be part of Zach's happiness. Sadly, it wasn't to be. Although, knowing he'd found his sister gave me peace. I'd longed for a sibling, but I was an only child. However, now I had a real tree family. Life wasn't perfect, but it was *pre-tree* dang good.

"Did you hear me?" Zelda demanded. "I said you smell stanky."

"Thank you," Zach replied.

"No, dumbass," Zelda insisted. "I mean it. You seriously need to shower. You smell like a huge butt."

"I repeat," Zach said, dryly. "Thank you."

"Duuuude, it was not a compliment."

Zach sighed dramatically. "You're a pain in my ass."

Zelda laughed and raised her middle finger. "That's what sisters are for."

"I didn't ask for a sister," he replied, raising his brow.

"Tough titties," Zelda shot back. "You either go up to the house and take a damn shower or I create a rainstorm with a shit-ton of soap in it."

"I really smell like butt?" Zach asked with a tired grin.

"Butt is a stretch," Zelda admitted. "However, it's not good. Even Fat Bastard and the boys said you were gamey."

"Your cats complained about the way *I smell?*" Zach asked with a laugh. "The hairy sons of a bitches rolled in something dead yesterday."

"It was skunks, and they're still alive," Zelda said with a shudder. "I doused those bulbous smack-talking feline idiots in so much douche they'll never forget it."

"I'm sorry," Zach said, squinting at his sister. "Did you just say you douched your cats?"

"Damn right, I did. I had to douche all three of my brain-challenged familiars," she said, rolling her eyes. "Douche works better than anything when dumbass cats decide to hit on a trio of female skunks. You have no clue how horrifying it was to buy six cases of douche at the store. I'm sure all of Assjacket thinks I have something wrong with my va-jay-jay."

Zach laughed and let his chin fall to his chest in defeat. "That was more information than I ever wanted to know in my life."

"I've got more where that came from," she threatened with a wide grin that was identical to her brother's. "And if you don't haul your ass up to the house, I'm gonna douche you and enjoy it."

"Fine," Zach said. "I'll shower. Will you stay till I get back?"

Zelda nodded.

"Promise?" he questioned.

"Witch's honor," she said. "I'd hug you, but I smell good."

With a snap of his fingers, Zach disappeared in a cloud of bright blue glittering smoke.

The timing of Zach's departure had been perfect. I could thank Zelda for saving my life, ask about Zorro, my best friend, and then haul ass out of wherever I was and start searching for my tes-tree-cles. Now that I knew my love was among the living, I could move on with a lighter heart. It would be a broken heart, but it would be a happy broken.

However, I'd always come back to visit my trees.

Sucking in a deep breath, I walked right out of the tree and back into the world.

"Holy shit on a hot tin roof," Zelda screamed in horror as I appeared in front of her. "Goddess in mom jeans, you're a hot mess."

"Nice to see you, too," I said, looking down at myself. Zelda was correct. I *was* a hot mess. However, I had an excuse. I'd been in a tree for a month. Thank Goddess, I hadn't popped out of the tree while Zach had still been here. I could deal with him not loving me, but I didn't want his pity.

With a wave of my hand, I cleaned up. Gone was the leafy dress and sappy smell. I was now in a bright green Alice and Olivia number and Prada wedges. My head wreath blossomed sparkling gold and pale pink flowers, and I smelled like a summer breeze.

"Better?" I asked with a grin.

"Much. And I'd like to put in an order for that dress in blue. Can you make that work, dryad?" she asked, grinning back.

"I believe I can, witch," I told her, waving my hands and granting her wish.

"Sassy will shit her pants that she wasn't here to get a new dress," Zelda said with a laugh as she twirled and modeled her new outfit. "So did my large wooden menaces fix you up?"

Trying out my legs and pacing around Sponge Bob, I nodded my head. "They did. Sponge Bob and I bonded. I hope that's okay with you."

Zelda wrinkled her nose. "Umm... define *bonded*."

I laughed at her alarmed expression. "He's my tree pappy —like a giant wooden father. I'm his baby tree-hugger."

Zelda blew out a wildly relieved breath and clapped her hands with delight. "Fucking perfect. You realize they're my minions, right?"

I nodded. "I do. You're lucky to have such brave and wonderful trees in your corner."

"Wait," Zelda said, pursing her lips. "Does that make us related somehow?"

Shrugging, I grinned. "Distan-tree, I suppose."

"Oh my Goddess in a muumuu," she said with a giggle and an eye roll. "You speak tree?"

"I do," I admitted, shaking my head. "I try to avoid Puntreelish at all costs, but hanging with the boys for a month made it all come back."

Zelda leaned in close. "I like it," she whispered. "Do not tell them, though. It's better if they think I'm an insane meanie with an obscene vocabulary."

"They call you Zelda of the Poopy Crap Mouth," I whispered back. "They adore you."

Her laugh rang out and the trees rustled with delight. "I

love it," she said, patting Sponge Bob's bark with affection. "However, you big wooden pain in my butt, if that ever gets around, I will chop your ass down and use you for firewood. Am I clear?"

"Yes, O' Beautiful Zelda of the Poopy Crap Mouth," Sponge Bob said with a chuckle as a few leaves fell from his branches and landed on Zelda's head.

Zelda brushed the leaves away and looked me over from head to toe. "So, you're really healed? Because if you're feeling iffy, I can repair anything the trees might have missed. As the Shifter Wanker, my specialty is accident-prone, furry numb-nuts, but I can help dryads too."

"I'm good. I'm great. And I'm alive thanks to you and the boys. I don't know how I can ever repay you for saving my life. Thank you, Zelda."

"You're welcome, Willow. It was a no fucking brainer. You're a kickass chick, and I'm stuck with tree minions. Win, win. However, I'd like to keep my rapidly eroding reputation of being an uncaring witch intact, so let's keep my good deed a secret," she said with a wink.

"My lips are sealed," I told her with a grin.

"So, here's the plan," Zelda said, snapping her fingers and conjuring up a notebook. "Keeping lists is more of a Sassy move, but there's so much shit going on in the shitshow right now, I can barely keep it straight. You feel me?"

I nodded in confusion. Zelda was a strange one with a healthy penchant towards mass destruction. Nodding was safest at this point. Even profane and violent, I really liked Zelda. I hadn't had any female friends for decades. Her best friend Sassy was missing a few brain cells, but I liked her too.

"Okay, try to follow me here," Zelda said, squinting at the pages in her book. "Babayoconebra took off on a girl's trip with her sister Cookie Witch, aka Marge, to stalk Madonna and Duran Duran. It's incredibly shitty timing since Fabio has been lurking in the woods, stalking Zach. Fabdudio also needs a damn shower. Bermanggoggleshitz, Sassy's dad, has been keeping Fabio company, which will lead to a no-good or possible illegal merger. And yes, Bermangoggleshitz is a gas-inducing last name, but Sassy mated with Jeeves, whose last name is Pants, making her *Sassy Pants*. When she discovered her father, she took his name as well. She's Sassy Bermangoggleshitz Pants now. She somehow thinks that's better," Zelda said with an eye roll that deserved an award.

I was mute and completely unsure how to react. It didn't matter. Zelda was on a roll.

"So, having Babayobadtiming and Marge out of town sucks. Everything might be solved if Zach wasn't acting like a shitball and would just acknowledge Fabio. Of course, my brother camping out under Sponge Bob for a month isn't making any kind of reunion easier. I'm in a pickle here because with all the stinky idiots roaming around my yard, I can't act out *Mermaid Does the Sexy Sea Monster* in the pool at night with Mac. I mean, with toddlers it's difficult to find nookie time. We could always go to the Floating Nookie Hut, but that would mean I'd have to leave the noxious turds in charge of my babies. My sex life is completely cramped by odoriferous warlocks and it's not working for me."

"I understood very little of that," I said, wondering if Sponge Bob would mind if I came back for a visit immediately. However, staying out in the real world was beginning to appeal to me. Maybe. "Umm... why was Zach camped out under Sponge Bob for a month?"

Zelda gave me an odd a look I couldn't quite decipher. My face heated with embarrassment, and I wanted to take the question back. It was too late.

"Guess you'll have to ask Zach," she said with a barely disguised grin. "Anyhoo, you'll see the big picture soon enough. The shining light is Zorro. Thank the Goddess he's here, or I would have turned my smelly pappy and reeking twin into toads and thrown them in the pond."

"Zorro's alive?" I asked, a little breathlessly pushing away my ridiculous wishful thinking about Zach's reasons for staying close to Sponge Bob. I leaned on my tree family so my knees didn't buckle. Life was very good right now. All three of us had survived. That was all that mattered. "And Zorro's here?"

"Yep. I swear on the Goddess's gauchos, Zorro's one hundred percent fine, and the town is in love with him."

The fact that Zorro was loved didn't surprise me one bit. He was kind, loyal and hilarious. However, it did lead to another question. "Where exactly are we?"

"Dude," Zelda said with a laugh. "You have some catching up to do. But to answer your question, we're in Assjacket, West Virginia."

I was pretty sure I'd heard her wrong. "Seriously?"

"No," she said with a shrug. "It's not technically Assjacket, but it's what I call it, and the name has kind of stuck. It's catchy and accurate."

"What's the real name of the town?" I asked, curious.

Zelda twisted her long red locks in her fingers and paused. "Honestly, I have no fucking clue, but as I said, Assjacket works perfectly."

I shrugged and smiled. "Got it. Assjacket it is. And is that your house on the hill?"

"Yep and yours too for as long as you'd like. But again, let's not let it get out that I invited you. Messes with the rep. Cool?"

Tilting my head, I stared at her in confusion. "I'm not staying."

It was Zelda's turn to look confused. "Of course, you are. You love Zach."

"Loved," I lied through my teeth. It was incredibly diffi-cult, but doable... and necessary. I did love Zach. The problem was that Zach only *liked* me. It was far past time to let go of unpractical fantasies that wouldn't come true. Ten years was long enough. It was time for a new dream. "I mean, I still care for him as a friend, but not in any other way."

Zelda was speechless. Even in the short time I'd known her, I knew this was a rare occurrence.

"Excuse me for a sec," she choked out as she walked about twenty feet from the trees.

With a clap of her hands and a slew of impressive profanities, she blew an enormous crater in the ground. The explosion shook the earth beneath my feet, and I leaned on the trees for balance. I briefly wondered if Zelda was putting in a pool, but I spotted a whole bunch of backyard pools and hot tubs in the distance. Maybe they loved swimming. Witches could be odd creatures.

"Are you okay?" I asked.

"Been better," she admitted. "However, blowing shit up is very calming. You should try it."

"I'll keep that in mind," I told her. "Can I see Zorro?"

Zelda nodded slowly. "Sure. He's staying with me, too. What about Zach? In fifteen minutes, he won't smell like a walking butt."

"Umm… possibly," I said as my stomach somersaulted. I felt like sprinting into the woods to begin my Mick Jagger way of life immediately. Hell, I'd even wear spandex if I had to.

"You also need to eat," she pointed out.

"I am kind of hungry," I admitted as my stomach growled in agreement.

"Do you like peanut butter and jelly with the bread in the middle?" Zelda inquired as she took my hand and began marching us toward her beautiful home.

"Never tried it like that," I said, testing her grip.

It was solid. I was going up to the house whether I wanted to or not.

"You'll love it," she promised. "My little ones make them. Kind of messy, but delicious. You in?"

I was pretty damn sure I didn't have a choice. Plus, I did need to say goodbye to Zorro… and Zach. If I was going to search for my metaphorical hairy magic beans, I couldn't whack them off at the beginning of the journey.

I was a grown dryad—a magical being with pride and confidence. I would wish the man of my dreams well and then leave him behind. If I couldn't have him, I didn't want to stand in the wings and watch some other lucky woman win his heart. Plus, I didn't need a man to be complete. I just needed to find me and my nards.

"I'm in."

CHAPTER THREE

"OH MY GODDESS, WHAT IS THAT *SMELL*?" I CHOKED OUT AS we approached the house.

Zelda and Mac's home was amazing—a beautiful and huge log cabin with a rustic wrap-around-porch nestled into the side of a tree-covered hill. I was sure I counted at least four chimneys coming out of the roof.

However, as lovely as the exterior might be, it smelled Goddess awful.

"Mother humper," Zelda shouted, slapping her forehead. "I'm so fucking embarrassed. My house doesn't normally smell like a giant ass. I guess the douche didn't work. My familiars, Fat Bastard, Jango Fett and Boba Fett got sprayed when they tried to become one with skunks yesterday. The smell got singed into my nasal cavity, and I hoped it was just me who could still smell it."

"Umm... nope," I said with a wince and a pained laugh. "I'll go on record and say the douche didn't work."

"I'm gonna have to get the jackholes waxed," she muttered. "It's about to get ugly here. Last time Sassy waxed my cats there was hell to pay. But that should teach the ball-licking freaks not to try to bang skunks ever again."

"One would hope," I said, wishing I could stay in this crazy place. As strange as it was, it was clearly filled with love and bizarre—albeit stinky—shenanigans.

"You want a nose plug?" Zelda offered. "I keep them around for when Bob the beaver Shifter eats magical berries."

I wasn't going to touch that one.

Shaking my head, no, I swallowed my laugh. "I'm good. I'll get used to it, I'm sure."

"Don't be too sure. It's freaking awful," she said with a grunt of disgust as she yanked me up the stairs to the front porch. "Zorro is going to faint when he sees you."

"To be expected," I said with a wide smile. "He is a fainting goat Shifter."

"And a very snazzy dresser," Zelda added as she opened the front door and pushed me through.

I'd stay for a bit to be polite. Zelda had saved my life, and I needed to show my appreciation. I'd meet her babies, eat a messy sandwich, say hello to Zorro, and then I'd say goodbye to Zach. It would be the closure I needed to move on.

"Well, hell's bells," Zelda said, looking around, perplexed. "Where is everyone?"

The massive great room was empty. It was also warm and inviting—all exposed beams, earthy colors and clean lines. Toys and stuffed animals littered the floor and tons of

26

natural light illuminated the lovely area. The house had a real sense of joy.

"Sit," Zelda directed as she pointed to the couch. "I'll find Zorro and the kids."

She moved to leave and then turned back quickly. "You won't make a run for it when I'm gone?"

The witch had my number, but I wasn't going to be a coward. "I'll stay for a little while. I promise."

"That's what I said when I got to Assjacket," she muttered as she left the room.

I had no clue what she was talking about, but figuring out Zelda could take decades. For now, I'd simply do as asked. A few hours wouldn't matter anyway. It could take me years to find my metaphorical gonads.

Feeling a little lightheaded about facing Zach, I leaned back on the couch and closed my eyes. I really did want the very best for him. I loved him, but he could never know. He'd lived a hell on earth for his entire existence. His new life should be guilt-free.

"Psssst," came a voice from underneath the couch. "Youse alone, hot pants?"

Gasping in surprise, I pinched my nose shut as a waft of skunk butt aroma wafted through the room. I tried not to gag. "Yes, I'm alone. Is that you, Fat Bastard?"

"Youse bet yer fine patooty it is," he grunted as he shimmied out from under the couch with immense effort.

Boba Fett and Jango Fett followed with as much difficulty as their buddy. The cats had enormous bellies and bottoms. And they reeked like nothing I'd ever encountered. Fat Bastard glanced around warily and moved in closer. I truly adored Zelda's familiars, just not right this minute. It was all I could do not to hurl. Breathing through my mouth so I didn't pass out, I smiled at the cats. I was sure it wasn't one of my best smiles, but I was making an effort.

"Do youse happen to have any douche on youse?" Fat Bastard asked.

"Umm… no," I told him with a choked laugh. "I don't usually carry douche."

"Shit don't work anyway," Boba Fett announced, falling back onto his bottom and lifting his hind kitty leg high in the air.

I turned my head away politely as he went to town on his odoriferous jewels.

"Hows about baking soda, peroxide and fish soap?" Jango Fett questioned.

"You mean dish soap?" I asked.

Jango shrugged his furry shoulders. "Youse say dish soap. I says fish soap. Same shit, different name. Youse got any? We'd be willin' to cut a deal for it."

"Nope, no douche or fish soap," I said, getting an idea. I'd never actually tried de-stinking cats, but I'd always been excellent at bringing back peace and harmony to forests and wildlife after natural disasters. The cats definitely qualified as natural disasters. "Would you guys mind if I took a crack at cleaning you up?"

"Youse wanna clean our cracks?" Fat Bastard looked wildly intrigued.

"I'd be into dat," Boba said, lifting his head from his socially unacceptable habit.

"My crack could use a good lickin'," Jango added, winking at me.

"Umm... no. Absolutely not. Never. I really don't want anything to do with your cracks," I said, shaking my head. "I was thinking more along the lines of removing the odor."

"From our cracks?" Fat Bastard asked, still not with the program.

"Well, I suppose your cracks would benefit," I conceded. "I think it might be less painful than getting waxed."

"Mother humpin' turd nuggets," Fat Bastard hissed. "Is dat the plan?"

"It's on the list of possibilities," I said, still pinching my nose so I didn't accidentally breathe through it. "If the three of you would line up, I can cast a little spell and it might solve the problem."

"Youse want our cracks facin' youse?" Boba asked as he waddled over.

"Definitely not," I told him. "Keep your cracks facing the other way."

"Don't see how youse is gonna lick our cracks if youse can't see our cracks," Jango muttered as he followed my directions.

"Is dis gonna hurt?" Fat Bastard inquired. "I like a good spankin' now and then, but dats as far as I go."

"I don't mind gettin' tied up and light floggin'," Jango informed me.

"Youse can spank me any day of de week," Boba overshared.

"Mmkay, all of that was TMI," I told them. "And no, it

won't hurt at all. I'm just not sure it will work. What's your favorite flower?"

Fat Bastard raised his little paw politely. "I'm partial to dat amorphophallus titanium. Looks like a big schlong."

Not to be topped, Jango Fett chimed in. "I like dat one, but I'm gonna go with a calla lily. Dat flower looks like it's got a schlong and a hooha. Very impressive."

"Nah," Boba Fett said. "I'm more into the rubus cockburnianus family of plants because of the word cock in the title."

I regretted my question immediately. "Alrighty then," I said, biting back my laugh so I didn't encourage them. "Do you like roses?"

No one said a word. Maybe flowers weren't their thing. I tried again. "How about the scent of pine trees?"

Fat Bastard nodded. "Dat's a good one. Dem cones look like Johnsons. I vote for pine wieners."

"Youse can count me in on pine peckers too," Jango volunteered.

"Yep, I'm in for a nice pine baloney pony," Boba added.

"Pine it is," I said, grinning. Zelda's cats were as profane as she was.

With a wave of my hand, an enchanted glistening pine-scented breeze floated through the massive room and wrapped the hairy ball lickers in a warm magical embrace.

"Tickles!" Fat Bastard said, giggling.

"Dis is niiiiiiice," Boba squealed as he jiggled with laughter.

"My crack is lovin' it!" Jango shouted as he shook with hysterics.

"Just another few seconds," I told them, letting my hand dance in the air and saying a quick prayer to the Goddess that it would work. I'd hate to see the cats get waxed.

Fat Bastard, Jango Fett and Boba Fett floated on the gentle wind and giggled with joy. Taking the risk of vomiting, I cautiously breathed in through my nose. Bingo. Skunk butt aroma gone. Clean forest pine scent in its place.

"Dat was infuckingcredible," Fat Bastard announced. "We owe youse, Willow."

Jango sniffed his privates and gave me a kitty thumbs up. "My crack smells delicious."

"Umm... great," I said with a wince. "Good to know."

"Youse de bomb!" Boba said. "The Bastard is correct. We owe youse. Whatever youse want, we will steal it for youse."

"Thanks, but no thanks," I told them. "I'm good."

"It also applies to a magical favor," Fat Bastard said, taking a whiff of his pits. "Weese would never welch on a favor to a pretty gal who fixed our cracks."

"I'll keep that in mind," I said, scratching their odor-free heads. "Just stay away from the skunks."

"Roger dat," Fat Bastard said as he purred with content. "Dem gals is too uppity anyway."

"Let's go make Zelda sniff our cracks," Boba suggested. "She's gonna freak."

"Thanks again, doll face," Fat Bastard said as the trio waddled out of the great room. "Don't forget, weese have yer back."

I waved and sighed in relief. My de-stinking the cats wasn't enough of a repayment for all that Zelda had done for me, but it was certainly a start.

Settling myself back on the couch, I leaned back and closed my eyes. I shouldn't be tired after a month of rest, but the anticipation of what was about to happen drained me. I'd just get through it. There was no other choice.

"Pssssst," came a different voice from behind the curtains.

What was it about this place? Did everyone hide?

"Can I help you?" I asked, glancing over at the moving curtain in alarm.

"Possibly," the male voice said.

It was a strangely familiar voice, but I couldn't place it.

"You want to come out from behind the curtain or are we playing *The Wizard of Oz*?" I inquired.

"Are you alone?" he asked.

Now I was getting a bit nervous. Was someone here to harm Zelda or her babies? Maybe Zorro or Zach? Not going to happen on my watch.

"I am," I said, standing up and ready to zap the hell out of anyone even slightly nefarious. "Come out and keep your hands at your sides. If you make a wrong move, it will be your last."

"Your balls are enormous," he commented. "That's wonderful."

"Umm… thank you," I said. "Actually, I lost them somewhere along the way. I'm currently searching for them."

"I disagree," he countered. "I'm pretty sure you're wearing them right now."

"Again, thank you," I said, pleased that the villain behind the curtain thought I had hairy magical beans. "And again, come out with your hands at your sides. Now."

"As you wish," he said, peeking out.

I almost swallowed my tongue. "Zach?" I shouted.

"No," he whispered, glancing around in fear. "I'm Fabio."

"You guys are triplets?" I asked, completely confused. I vaguely remembered Zelda saying something about Fabio and Bermangoggleshitz lurking in the woods and stalking Zach. She'd seemed unconcerned by it, but I didn't like the thought of Zach being stalked by anyone.

Fabio's smile was identical to Zach's and Zelda's. His bright green eyes twinkled and his dark auburn hair stood on end. It looked as if he'd run his hands through it a hundred times. The man was clearly not a villain. However, who he was to Zach and Zelda remained to be seen. I had an idea, but needed confirmation.

"Who exactly are you, Fabio?" I asked, eyeing him suspiciously.

"I'm Zelda and Zach's father," he whispered, his eyes darting to the staircase.

"And you're hiding behind the curtain because?"

"Well, I'm not exactly wanted at the moment... by Zach," he admitted sadly. "I'm working on it."

"By hiding in the curtains?" I pressed, thinking that was an odd way to work on it. Although, witches and warlocks were an unusual breed.

"Can we talk?" he asked with a smile so charming I smiled right back. "I'd like to get to know you."

"Yes." Admittedly, I was curious about Fabio, so I agreed to the chat. "Yes, we can."

CHAPTER FOUR

"I LOCKED ZACH IN THE BATHROOM WITH THE CATS AND Zorro—even put a complicated spell on the door," Zelda said, balancing her toddler daughter Audrey on one hip and her son Henry on the other while grinning from ear to ear. She was positively crazy. But the more I learned about her, the more I liked. Apparently, she had overheard Fabio and me in the great room and felt it necessary to lock her brother in the bathroom with her pine-scented cats and my BFF Zorro displaying his bare bottom.

Why? I hoped to find out.

She nodded at me and continued. "We have about a half hour. I told Zorro to detain Zach as well. The goat is modeling his assless chaps. Zach is probably dying a slow death right now."

"Great," I said, still very confused by the whole hostage situation going on in her bathroom.

"First of all, thank you for de-stinking my idiotic cats,"

35

Zelda said. "They're all keen on me sniffing their cracks. I told the furry dorks if they kept insisting on me getting even within two feet of their cracks, I'd permanently remove them."

A laugh burst from my lips. I realized I'd laughed more today than I had in a long time. "You're most welcome for the de-stinking. It's the least I could do. As for the crack part, they misunderstood something I said."

"Typical. They're not the sharpest tools in the shed," Zelda said, handing Audrey to a delighted Fabio and plopping Henry into my lap.

Her children were so adorable, and I'd been itching to hold them. The little boy looked right into my eyes, smiled and blew a raspberry. Henry then stuck his thumb into his mouth, cuddled close and fell asleep in my arms. Heaven.

"I'm just going to dive right in here due to limited time. Fabio banged my pathetic excuse for a mother, and she got knocked up," Zelda began.

"I had no clue she was pregnant," Fabio volunteered quickly. "I was a bit of a man whore at the time."

"Man whoreeeeeee!" Audrey yelled as Fabio blanched in horror.

"Sorry," he whispered.

Zelda shook her head and grunted in pain. "You will explain that one to Mac," she informed her father. "He will kick your sorry ass."

"Assssssssssss," Henry grunted sleepily. "My daddy kicky your asssssssssss."

Snapping his fingers, Fabio conjured up a roll of duct tape and tossed it to his daughter.

Catching it, she nodded her thanks. "I have three strikes. I've only used one," she said. "Plus, we have to get Willow up to speed quickly."

Feeling their panic, I curled Henry closer, sat up straighter, and paid close attention. Having no clue what else I was going to hear, I didn't want to miss any details.

"Okay," Zelda continued. "To make a long fuc...arrked up story short. When Fabio found out about me, he confronted my piece of poopoo egg donor, and she cast a poopy doody spell on him and turned him into a cat."

"Right," Fabio agreed. "The poopy dookie spell..."

"I said *doody* not *dookie*," Zelda pointed out. "Although, dookie is more satisfying,"

Fabio raised his brow at his daughter.

"Keep going," she hissed. "I was giving you a compliment on the dookie thing, jackhole."

"Thank you, Zelda," Fabio said with a grin. "Anyhoo, the horrid dingleberry of a woman turned me into a cat, and I had to earn Zelda's love in order to revert back to myself."

"So, get this," Zelda said, shaking her head. "I find him in a dumpster and the mangy fart pebble of cat followed me home."

"Where you ran over me with your butt fudge car," Fabio added.

"It was a peepeeing accident," Zelda said with an eye roll.

"All three times, diaper breath?" Fabio inquired with a laugh.

"Yessssssssssss, hiney face," Zelda insisted, laughing with him.

This family was insane and wonderful.

"Although, to your credit and excellent taste, you did bury me in a Prada shoebox," Fabio recalled.

"With the shoe bags as a pillow and blanket, boom-boom mouth," she reminded him.

"Nice touch," I said with a giggle. "Can either of you work pooplet or hot sloppy into a sentence?"

"I like you," Fabio said, giving me a lopsided grin and a nod of approval.

"Right?" Zelda said. "Willow's perfect. Unlike the hot sloppy locked in the bathroom at the moment."

Fabio anxiously glanced over at the stairs. "Speaking of... hurry up, pooplet. We don't have much time."

"You guys are awesome," I said with a laugh.

Zelda nodded and smiled. "I certainly think so. But back to the horrifying history lesson, after the hit and run incident, I got incarcerated for mowing down my familiar—who wasn't actually dead, obviously—among other things that we won't go into."

"She got jailed for using magic for self-serving purposes," Fabio chimed in unhelpfully as far as Zelda was concerned.

"Oh my Goddess," Zelda griped at her father. "All the details are not important, stink bomb."

"My bad, BM," he replied.

"I should say so, caca," she snapped at her dad.

"Diaper fillers," I interjected. "Finish the story."

"Ohhh, I like that one," Zelda said with a thumbs up.

"You're welcome," I told her.

"Okay, after I got sprung from the pokey in Salem where I was roommates with Sassy, I was given a mission in Assjacket. My dead cat was in the car on the drive down."

"Wasn't dead anymore," Fabio pointed out. "You know, nine lives and all that stuff."

"Got it," I said. "Keep talking."

Zelda paced the room and continued. "Right. I got here. Hated it, but secretly loved it. Became the Shifter Wanker. Banged the King of the Shifters, fell in love and got knocked up."

"There's more," Fabio said. "As I was dying after Zelda smacked down on some bad guys, she told me she loved me and I reverted back to myself."

"And he was *naked*," Zelda said with an enormous gag. "Never ever look at your pappy's pecker. I've been in therapy for years."

"My parents are gone," I said. It didn't hurt like an open wound anymore, but it still made me sad to say it.

"I'm so sorry," Fabio said softly.

"They were wonderful, and I'll always miss them," I told him. "But it was a very long time ago."

"I'm sorry," Zelda said, walking over to the couch and sitting down next to me.

I smiled. "Me too. I actually followed most of your story, but I still don't understand where Zach fits in or why Fabio was hiding behind the curtains."

"You're aware that my egg donor sold Zach as a baby to the ass-pipe who tried to kill you guys, right? And that Zach and I are twins?" she asked.

"I am," I said, looking down at the sleeping boy in my arms and wondering how any mother could sell her child. I was sure Zach looked very much like Henry as a baby. His wild dark red curls were so sweet.

"I didn't know about Zach, and Fabio didn't know about either of us. Zach's and my childhoods were bad," Zelda said, giving her father a look that conveyed she didn't blame him. "Problem we're having now is that Zach wants nothing to do with Fabdudio."

"Why?" I asked. I'd give anything to have my parents back in my life.

Zelda took a long pause and then sighed. "To love other people, you have to love yourself first."

I was stunned to silence for a moment. My heart tore a little for Zach. "That is seriously profound," I said.

"Got it from my porno loving rabbit Shifter therapist. Most of the time, I want to headbutt Roger, but the nose twitching little number-two is right fairly often. However, I will deny saying that for eternity."

"His name is Roger the rabbit?" I asked with a grin.

"Yep," Zelda said, gently taking Henry from my arms. "You're gonna love him. You might even want to do a few sessions with him. The little shart has helped me tremendously."

"You mean *tree-mendously*," I corrected her with a small laugh then let my chin drop to my chest. "But I really can't stay Zelda. I have to *leaf*, I mean leave."

"And go where?" Fabio demanded, alarmed.

"To find my hairy magical beans," I replied with a sad smile. "I lost them somewhere along my life journey."

"Will you give us a week before you search for your *tes-tree-cles*?" Fabio begged with a sweet smile.

"You speak Puntreelish?" I asked with a laugh.

"A little," he said. "I'd love to learn some more. Will you please stay a week?"

"You haven't had a peanut butter and jelly sandwich with the bread in the middle yet," Zelda pointed out.

"And you must see Zorro in his show," Fabio added.

"His show?" I asked, confused.

"He's starring in the Assjacket Community Theatre production of *Zorro, the Gay Blade—the Musical*," Zelda informed me with a groan.

"Actually," Fabio chimed in. "They changed the show."

"Why?" Zelda asked. "Zorro was thrilled with his part. That's why he bought the pink leather assless chaps."

Fabio rocked a sleeping Audrey in his arms and shook his head. "Apparently, a famous director with an entourage of height impaired ladies has all of a sudden shown up in town. She's insisted on changing the show to *Jaws—The Musical.*"

"You're shitting me. *Jaws* as a musical?" I asked and then slapped my hand over my mouth, hoping neither toddler woke up and repeated me.

"No, I'm not bowel movement-ing you," Fabio said.

"Wait. Who was supposed to direct?" Zelda asked, confused.

"Bob and the cast were going experimental and letting the play direct itself this time," Fabio said with a chuckle. "Maybe it's good this director showed up. I can't even imagine what a musical version of *Jaws* will turn out like, though." He shook his head. "Zorro is playing the shark in pink leather assless chaps. Poor Bob the beaver is trying to write the new script, but from what I hear, it's not going well. He's pulled more than half of his unibrow out."

"That had to hurt," I said with a wince, mulling all the information over. "Wait, is Bob the magical berry tooter?"

"Yep," Zelda said. "If you spot him with a bowl of berries, steer clear. However, Bob's butt bombs are nothing compared to how Zorro must be feeling."

My body tensed. "What do you mean?"

"Zorro has to be devastated about the show change," Zelda said. "Breaks my heart."

Crap. It was not okay for Zorro to be devastated.

"I'll stay… for a week," I said. The words came out of my mouth before I could think them through, but I would stand by them. If Zorro needed me, I would be here to comfort him.

Zelda and Fabio exchanged a glance of enormous relief. They were up to something, but at this point, I assumed they were always up to something. My concern was Zorro…and if I was being honest, Zach as well.

Zorro, my beautiful best friend, had been through hell in his life, too. Being a gay goat Shifter who'd been excommunicated from his pack, because goats were homophobic assholes, was painful enough. I'd stay until *Jaws* was over and cheer my most loyal friend on.

Of course, I would definitely see Zach, also, but that was secretly thrilling.

And then I would go off to find my balls.

"Welcome to Assjacket." Fabio gently laid a sleeping Audrey down on the couch then wrapped his arms around me.

The hug was lovely. It made me miss my own father. Maybe, I could help Zach accept Fabio. It would be a perfect parting gift to the man I secretly loved.

"Get your hands off of her," Zach bellowed from the bottom of the stairs. "Never touch her again. Willow is not available."

"Dude, Fabio is not *hitting* on Willow," Zelda hissed at her brother. "He's banging the fashion impaired leader of the witches much to my great horror and barley concealed secret delight. Plus, this is my house, and *you* are not the boss of it."

Zach's eyes blazed green and his fury was palpable. The air was thick with magic. Bright green sparks popped all around him, and the house rumbled on its foundation.

Fabio quickly backed away from me with an expression of great sadness on his handsome face.

"Zach, that wasn't nice," I barked, eyeing him with shock. My instinct was to comfort him, but that wasn't our relationship. Never had been and never would be.

"Do I look like I care?" he demanded.

"No, you don't," I said sadly. "And that's your loss."

"Willow," he said, approaching me warily with a look of longing in his eyes that confused me. "You have no clue what is going on. Please stay out of it."

"With pleasure," I said, backing away, wildly unsure what had come over Zach. "I'm only staying for a week to see Zorro in his play."

Zach looked crushed. "Is that the only reason?"

Misconstruing Zach's expression could end in massive public humiliation—specifically mine. Crossing my fingers and tucking my hands into the pockets of my dress, I nodded and lied. "Zorro is the only reason I'm staying for a week."

"Guurrlfriend!" Zorro squealed with joy as he came barreling down the stairs with the pine-scented cats on his heels. My beautiful BFF was in one solid piece and as handsome as ever. His vertical pupils set in bright blue eyes could be off-putting, but I found them exotic and cool—he was a fainting goat Shifter after all. Zorro's sandy blond hair fell over one eye, styled expertly. He grabbed me and swung me around like a doll. "You're alive! Best day ever."

Holding tightly to my best friend, I was torn between laughter and tears. Zorro had missed the showdown between Zach and Fabio. Maybe that was a good thing. He and Zach were also very tight.

"Best day ever," I whispered as he stopped spinning me and hugged me close.

It was and it wasn't. But Zorro was alive. Zach was alive. And I was alive. It was good enough for now.

"Will you come to my rehearsal?" Zorro asked.

I glanced over at Zach who stared right back at me. I was tempted to yank him up by his boxer briefs and tell him he was being an idiot about his family. Instead, I turned back to Zorro.

"I'd love to go to rehearsal with you." I winced at his pink leather assless chaps. "Are you wearing those pants?"

"Absolutely, guurrlfriend!" He wiggled his butt at me. "Helps me get into character."

"As the shark?" I asked with a giggle.

"I will be a shark like no other," Zorro promised with a wink as he walked me out to the front porch.

Understatement of the century.

Looking over his shoulder to make sure we were alone, Zorro pressed his forehead to mine and sighed. "I didn't know if you would make it."

"I made it," I said, swiping at a tear. "We all did."

Zorro inspected me from head to toe, then nodded in satisfaction. "Guurrlfriend, I prayed to the Goddess so hard while you were in the tree, she must be sick of me." He laughed and shook his head. "Zach was a straight-up hot mess. Had to force-feed him for a few weeks."

Zorro had always been the caretaker. While Henrietta Smith had mostly gone after Zach's blood, Zorro had taken the brunt of her voracious hunger when Zach was near death. Both men had tried to protect me from the abomination, but I'd taken my share of hits to relieve the horrific burden on the two men who meant the world to me. The fact that we were alive and Zach was free of the curse stole my breath.

"Everything is going to be alright now," Zorro said with a wide grin.

I nodded and smiled. I'd tell him later that I wasn't staying. Right now, I was living in the moment.

And the moment was as lovely as the smile on Zorro's sweet face.

CHAPTER FIVE

According to the sign in the lobby, the community center was used for the Assjacket Community Theatre, the Assjacket Cloggers, the Assjacket Hot Yoga Club, the Assjacket Knitting Circle, the Assjacket Book Club, the Assjacket Curling Society, and the Assjacket Assjackians. I was curious about what the Assjacket Assjackians did, but realized some things were better left up to the imagination.

"Is this a joke?" I whispered to Sassy as we sat in the back row of the cavernous room and watched the shitshow unfold on the built-in stage.

I'd successfully avoided Zach like the plague and slipped out of the house with Zorro. I was still mad and sad that Zach had been such a wanker to his father even though my entire body tingled when he was near. The time would come for us to talk, but now I was here for Zorro.

Bob the beaver—with a sad and sparse looking unibrow —ran around the large room with a sheaf of paper in his hands, talking to himself a mile a minute. Roger the rabbit sat at the piano and plunked out tune after tune about how it felt to get eaten by a shark in graphic detail. Zorro stood off to the left of the piano, looking like he was in the ninth level of hell as a few other Assjackians zipped around looking terrified and lost.

"Nope," Sassy said. "It's a catastro-tree. That's French for huge fucking mess."

I giggled. "Actually, it was Puntreelish."

"Shut the front door," Sassy said with wide eyes and a wider smile. "I'm speaking a new language?"

"You are," I told her. "It the language of the dryads and the trees."

"You know," she said, lowering her voice and putting her stiletto clad feet up on the row of chairs in front of us. "Sometimes, my excrement knowledge of language makes me feel like I'm almost smart. I mean, I know I'm not, but it's good to aspirate to greatness. I've tried for months to learn Canadian, and I can't understand a dang word of it."

"Sassy," I said, taking her hand and trying not to laugh. "You're very smart in lots of different ways. From what I hear, you're a wonderful mom to your adopted chipmunk Shifter sons and you can ride a broom like a professional."

"I love riding my broom! Works best commando—that's German for no panties. Did you know that?" she inquired with a naughty grin.

"Nope, but I do now," I said with a laugh. "Are you in the show?"

"I was," she said, looking forlorn. "I'm not sure if I am anymore since they changed it to *Jaws*. Last year I starred in

48

the musical version of *Mommie Dearest*. I was Christina, and I was amazeballs. I killed the number *No More Wire Hangers*."

I nodded because I wasn't sure how to react to that one.

"Where's the famous director?" I asked, glancing around.

"She's late and not fashionably. She showed up out of nowhere yesterday with her little troll-y looking entourage and changed the show," Sassy said with an eye roll. "I don't see the big deal. She's about two feet tall and mean as a snake."

"What is she?" I asked.

"A bitch," Sassy replied. "That's Swedish for heinous cow sphincter."

"Right," I said. "But is she a witch? Or a Shifter? Or something else?"

"Shifter... I think," Sassy said. "No one knows for sure what she or her nasty lady barnacles are, which is odd, but they're hideous—they wear black socks with sandals—all of them."

"You lie," I gasped out.

"Witch's honor," Sassy said with a shudder. "I screamed in horror when I saw them, but since I want a part, I pretended my nail polish was chipped."

"Excellent move," I said. Black socks and sandals were a fashion crime that warranted imprisonment.

I was now curious to see the cow patty and her cronies who had caused all this distress.

"Hey, am I late?" Zach asked as he breezed in and sat down next to Sassy.

"Late for what?" I asked, squinting at him in surprise. "Are you in the show?"

"Nope," he said, giving me a grin that made me a little breathless. "Thought I'd support Zorro."

Sassy's head went back and forth during the exchange. Her grin grew wide and she nudged me with her elbow. "He likes you," she whispered loudly.

"As a friend," I muttered as I felt Zach's intense stare. "We're old friends."

"Riiiight," Sassy said with a giggle. "You want me to talk to him for you? I'll be excrete."

"You mean discreet?" I asked as Zach listened to the exchange with interest.

"No," she said, shaking her blond curls. "Excrete is British for discreet. I was being fancy. British is a tricky language, but I've aced it. All you have to do to understand it is drink tea. I fucking hate tea, but I'm very dedicated to my world language quest. But back to the important stuff, I can send him a note with boxes on it. If he marks the *yes box,* it means he likes you. If he marks the *no box,* he's a dumbass. If he marks the *hermaphrodite box,* you should date someone else."

"Sassy, he's sitting right next to you," I pointed out, wanting to disappear.

She rolled her eyes. "Guys are idiots. He has no clue we're even talking about him. No worries. I have your back."

Zach bit down on his kissable bottom lip so he didn't laugh. I was mortified. Smacking both of them right now seemed like an excellent plan.

"She's coming! They're all coming!" Bob shrieked, pulling out what was left of his unibrow. "Everyone, sit down in the house. Cast stay on the stage. She read the first draft of the script last night and will give us her notes and brilliant words of wisdom."

All smackdowns would have to wait. The *famous director* and her troll-y entourage of mini-mes arrived. A strange dark pall came over the room as they entered. My gut clenched for a second and I tried to place the feeling.

Sassy and Zach didn't seem to notice.

Maybe I imagined it. I'd been in a tree for a month and was still a little fuzzy. However, there was no mistaking that the vibe in the room had changed and taken a turn towards the weird.

The famous director, Mae Blockinschlokinberg, stood no more than four feet and was as wide as she was tall. She wore a frock that looked like a muumuu made from chartreuse sweatpant material, and her black socks and beige sandals were shocking.

Zorro was hyperventilating and had grabbed onto the piano so he didn't pass out. Danger and horrific fashion choices were two things that made my fainting goat Shifter buddy lose consciousness. Mae Blockinschlokinberg's black socks and sandals were clearly too much for Zorro to handle.

Her minions looked like even more disgusting versions of their leader, and they were playing obsessively on their phones.

The squat disaster of a director walked to the center of the stage. She nodded jerkily at her four bizarre looking little followers who were huddled in a clump and taking pictures of her with their phones. Then, the gross woman pointed at Bob the beaver who shook like a leaf.

Bob cleared his throat for a minute and a half. He desperately searched for more unibrow to pull out and came up empty. With a gulp of terror, he finally spoke. "Ladies and gentlemen, I present to you Mae Blockinschlokinberg—the famed director of the musical *Showgirls*, the mimed production of *Starship Troopers* and of course, the twelve-hour interactive naked production of *Teenage Mutant Ninja Turtles*. We are blessed, terrified and shocked beyond belief that Mae Blockinschlokinberg has graced Assjacket with her brilliance and artistry."

"Naked production of *Teenage Mutant Ninja Turtles*?" Zach grunted quietly with a laugh.

"Took the words right out of my mouth," I whispered with a giggle. "However, I'm more curious about the mimed version of *Starship Troopers*."

Zach's grin made me tingle and feel strange inside. He'd always been kind to me—always been a loyal friend. However, this felt different.

Idiot. I was an idiot. My *friend* Zach was happy and relieved I was alive. Just like I was happy he was alive. Reading more into it was pitiful. He'd had ten years to make a move and hadn't.

Sassy turned her back to Zach and leaned into me. "He's not a hermaphrodite," she informed me. "I have a radar for that."

"You have a hermaphrodite radar?" I asked, wondering how insane Sassy truly was.

"Yes," she confirmed. "If someone smells like a calla lily,

they can do themselves. It's the flower with a schlong and a va-jay-jay. It's Canadian for, *I can bang myself so I don't need a significant other.*"

"Umm… I thought you didn't speak Canadian," I choked out, losing my battle with holding in a laugh.

"Just a few words," Sassy told me. "The guy sitting next to me who has no clue we're talking about him is not a calla lily."

"Good to know," I said, avoiding Zach's amused gaze for all I was worth.

Also, Sassy's insanity was confirmed. She was batshit nuts, and I enjoyed the heck out of her. However, she needed to quit the matchmaker job. She sucked.

"Attention," Mae Blockinschlokinberg shrieked in a voice that could break glass. "I have a few words to say to you lowly underlings."

"Silence!" Bob bellowed. He'd graduated to plucking the hair on his head since he'd demolished his unibrow. "The great one speaks."

Mae Blockinschlokinberg paced the stage as her four icky lackeys oohed and ahhed.

Again, I felt an uncomfortable foreboding sensation in my gut. Again, my radar could be skewed. It was definitely skewed—it seemed as if Zach was flirting with me. Ridiculous. I needed my head examined.

The director glared at poor Bob. Her beady eyes narrowed to slits. "No one is to make eye contact with me. No one is to disagree with me. And I need a snack table with eye of newt, tacos and Mountain Dew. Am I clear?"

Mae Blockinschlokinberg was a nasty piece of work.

That had to be the reason for the icky feelings. I disliked people like her.

"Yes, your majesty," Bob said bowing.

"What the heck is happening here?" I muttered. "That woman is an ass-pipe."

"I love that word," Sassy whispered. "Is it Puntreelish?"

"No, it's Pissedoffish," I replied. "Learned it from Zelda and thought it fit."

"It fits perfectly," Zach said, eyeing the woman with disgust.

Mae Blockinschlokinberg was just getting started. "So, beaver," she said with a sneer. "I published your play to Cramanon last night."

"WHAT?" Bob shrieked. "It was a rough first draft. It was nowhere near ready for publication."

"Silence," Mae Blockinschlokinberg snapped. "It's your punishment for not pleasing me. After I published it under your name, I reported it."

Mae Blockinschlokinberg's foul posse cackled like idiots and hung on the disagreeable woman's every word.

Bob paled and yanked most of the hair out of the left side of his head. "But... but... but I..."

"But nothing," she snapped. "All great art is developed in humiliation, drunkenness, constipation and misery. I have helped you, you pathetic tree gnawer."

"Total heinous cow sphincter," I whispered.

"You're speaking Swedish," Sassy whispered back.

"Yep," I said with a small grin. "Thanks to you, I am."

"I barely know the guy, and I want to rescue him," Zach

said angrily. "I have half a mind to cover that abomination in boils."

"Boils might be an improvement," I muttered.

"As fun as that would be, don't do it," Sassy advised. "It would mess up the play, and the whole town would be devastated."

"Explain," Zach said through clenched teeth as he watched the horrible little woman terrify the masses.

"Okay," Sassy said. "It's like this, it's totally cool to lose your shit because someone is being a dickwad. And I understand that if you hold your shit inside, you could become full of shit and then explode like a bomb and there will be shit everywhere—a shitstorm so to speak, which is the Hawaiian word for a stinky doody pile. And, I just don't see how everyone covered in poopoo would help right now."

"Sassy, you're going to have to do better than that," Zach said, closing his eyes and trying not to laugh.

"Right. I'll speak a language you can understand. Hawaiian is difficult. I'll speak British," she said with a nod. "They already paid Mae Blockinschlokinberg the entire budget for two years. If there's no show, the Assjacket Community Theatre will be ruined and become the laughing stock of the Tennessee Man-Titty Thespians. *No one* wants to be laughed at by the Tennessee Man-Titty Thespians. It's a fate worse than death, according to Bob."

Zach winced. "Sassy, is that really what they're called? Seems kind of politically incorrect."

"What? Thespians? Did you think I said Lesbian Man-Titties? Because I can see how that would be bad. Lesbians have woman-titties. So, no, I didn't say Lesbian," she explained to an aghast Zach.

"Umm… no," I said, helping Zach out and digging the Sassy hole deeper. There was no telling what could come out of her mouth next. "The man-titties part."

"Nope, that part is true," she told us. "They have big bouncy man hooters."

"Got it," Zach said. "Very visual."

Sassy nodded. "Thank you. I'm good like that. Anyhoo, Bob and Roger think the little blob is brilliant. I personally think they ate too many magical berries. However, as bulbous and disgusting as Mae Blockinschlokinberg is—which is Spanish for fucking wiener-faced skank folds fungus—if she gets fired, she'll keep the money and we have no play. And on top of that stinky news, Bob is up for some international communist theatre award for this show. He says his life will be complete if he wins."

"There's an international *communist* theatre award?" I asked, confused.

"Totally," Sassy confirmed. "The winner gets an all-expense-paid trip to a motel forty miles from the Jersey shore and a lifetime supply of ticket rolls to use for upcoming productions."

I was speechless.

Zach was not. "Not sure the prize merits the abuse," he said, eyeing the squat terror on the stage with disgust. "I'm done standing by when people are getting hurt."

I was very aware of what he was talking about. He'd had no control when he was under the curse and had helplessly watched as Henrietta Smith had harmed and killed others.

The curse had blocked him from stopping her. It had been a heavy load to carry. Zorro and I knew he hadn't been at fault, but I also knew that Zach didn't believe it.

"Can you do it and not get caught?" Sassy asked with an excited gleam in her eyes.

Zach's smile grew wide. "Yes. Yes, I can."

"Go for it," Sassy said. "But make it look real, not like magic."

"Not. A. Problem," Zach said, sinking lower in his seat and waiting for an opening.

I was sure something was about to go very wrong, but I was all in for the plan. Mae Blockinschlokinberg was asking to be taken down a peg or two or ten. Her mere presence was vile. I sat back and waited for the show to start.

"Here's what I reported to Cramanon from your abomination of a play, beaver," she said with a snarky smile that looked as if she had gas. "No one drinks red wine with salmon. Ever. That was a horrifying faux pas. I was appalled and reported it five times."

"I drink red wine with salmon," I hissed. "She's way behind."

"You got that right," Sassy agreed. "I drink red wine with peanut butter and jelly. It's awesome."

Bob was crushed. Mae Blockinschlokinberg was on a vicious roll.

"Southern accents are rubbish. I went through the entire script and corrected and reported all the upsetting vernacular," she said with a delighted sneer. "You'll receive a quality notice on Cramanon due to my superior knowledge of grammar. You *might* even lose your publishing privileges."

"I hate her so bad," Sassy grumbled. "Who does she think she is? Bob wrote an amazing script when they did the musical version of *Silence of the Lambs*. Sadly, it was before I lived in Assjacket. I would have been incredible in that show. Rumor has it that several audience members got kind of eaten and the Fava Bean number was lewd, but everyone says it was really good. Bob takes his playwriting very seriously."

"Are you serious?" I choked out. "How do people get *kind of eaten*?"

"Oh, you know," Sassy said with a shrug. "An arm, a leg— it all worked out because they were Shifters. Stuff grows back. So, it's clear how amazeballs Bob is, which really makes me want to smite that swollen dung humper right out of town."

"She's quite hate-able," Zach agreed. He wiggled his fingers as Mae Blockinschlokinberg walked back to the center of the stage. "Has the old bag ever even written a play?"

"My guess would be no," I said, watching the stage to see what magic Zach had done. "What did you do?"

"Wait for it," Zach said with a grin.

Bob raised his hand to speak. "I don't understand why you would do this. The play takes place in the South per your request. It's how we speak," Bob said in a shaky voice. "I could be ruined. My playwriting career could be over. Why would you try to ruin me?"

Mae Blockinschlokinberg laughed like a maniac and pointed a boney finger at Bob. "Because I can," she shouted and stamped her foot.

The stage caved in with a crash, and she fell right through it. It wasn't a huge fall, but it was fabulously loud and humiliating. She deserved much worse. Her little minions screamed in horror, yet made no move to save her. However, they did take a few pictures. So much for the trolls having her back.

"Bingo." Zach grinned.

"I like it." Sassy gave him a thumbs up. "Should we blow her up now?"

"Nope," Zach said. "Small annoyances will drive her crazy. Stay subtle, Sassy."

"Got it," she said, waving her hand. Mae Blockinschlokinberg was now bald... and pissed.

"Umm... that wasn't exactly subtle," I said with a giggle.

"Shit. Is subtle a Canadian word?" Sassy asked. "I thought it was the Mid-western word for hairless."

"No, it actually means understated," I told her.

"I don't speak Russian," she said in all seriousness.

"Mmkay... subtle means unnoticeable or tiny. Itty bitty magic," I explained.

"Balls, my bad," Sassy said, waving her hand and giving Mae Blockinschlokinberg her hair back with a little bit extra.

Mae Blockinschlokinberg now had a bushy unibrow that rivaled Bob's before he'd plucked all the hairs out. It was incredibly disturbing since Sassy had matched it perfectly to her nasty beige sandals.

"Subtle, huh?" Sassy asked with a wicked grin.

"Very," I lied with a laugh.

Roger the rabbit screamed like a little girl and began choking... or laughing. I couldn't be sure.

Bob ran to the nightmare and pulled her out of the hole.

"I'm so sorry. We'll have the stage reinforced immediately," he whimpered. His eyes grew huge when he spotted Mae Blockinschlokinberg's new beige unibrow. He glanced wildly around the room, and Sassy waved at him like a dummy.

Grabbing Sassy's arm, I yanked it down. "That's not subtle," I told her.

"Crap," she said, shaking her head. "Itty bitty magic is hard."

"See that you fix the stage, you worthless beaver," Mae Blockinschlokinberg snarled and then continued her diatribe of mean. "I also reported you for a missing quotation mark, an absentee comma and using the word *to* with one O instead of two. Completely ruined my reading experience."

I barely knew any of these people, but they seemed kind and didn't deserve this foul treatment. No one deserved Mae Blockinschlokinberg's toxic assault.

"Enough," I said, standing up and walking toward the stage. "This behavior is unacceptable."

"Agreed," Zach growled, coming up right next to me.

"Hell to the yes!" Sassy yelled as she pulled a broom out from underneath her chair and began to fly around the hall.

I hoped she was wearing panties, but there were more important things to deal with at the moment.

"You *dare* to backtalk me?" Mae Blockinschlokinberg snapped, eyeing Zach and me with great interest.

Her little group of losers pointed at us and whispered frantically—snapping pictures a mile a minute. It seemed as if old Mae Blockinschlokinberg wasn't fond of being called out and her little ladies didn't like it either.

"Yep, and I won't sit and watch nice people get treated so horribly," I said, staring right back at the nasty little woman. I'd had more than enough of her attitude. I also had some money in the bank—not a lot because dryads didn't need much, but hopefully enough to cover a community theatre budget in Assjacket, West Virginia and keep it from being shut down by the heinous hack.

"I'll stop your abuse if necessary," Zach told her, his tone icy.

"And I'm a member of the Fashion Police. You are in *huge* fucking trouble, Mae Blockinschlokinberg," Sassy yelled.

"Excellent!" the nasty woman shouted, making everyone in the room jump. She glanced over at her minions who nodded spastically. "You're all cast. Your balls are just what this play needs. Good work, beaver. I didn't think you had it in you. Congratulations."

"What?" Bob asked, wildly confused.

"I'll be back at four," Mae Blockinschlokinberg announced. "I expect everyone to know their lines for act one. It will be a mind-blowing gender-bender version of *Jaws*. It will be my shining moment as a director! Willow." She pointed at me. I found it strange that she knew my name. "You will play the sheriff as a man. Zach, you will perform the marine biologist as a woman. You, on the broom, you will be the captain, and you will be a hermaphrodite. Bob, make sure to write in a love triangle…

61

actually make it a foursome with Zorro the shark. My brilliance astounds me."

Everyone was shocked into stunned silence. Zorro passed out then hopped right back to his feet. Thankfully his fainting spells were quick.

"So, umm… we're shit-canning the actual story of *Jaws?*" Bob choked out in a strangled whisper.

"We're improving it," Mae Blockinschlokinberg said with a crazed expression of joy on her tiny mean face. "Learn your lines!"

On that note, Mae Blockinschlokinberg and her attendants waddled out of the building.

"What the hell just happened?" Zach asked, squinting at me.

"I have no idea," I said with a shudder. "It all happened so fast."

Bob walked over and stuck out his hand. "Welcome to the show," he said, looking like he wanted to cry.

Taking his trembling hand in mine, I shook it. The little man pulled at my heartstrings. "I'm Willow. It's nice to meet you, Bob, I think. Would you mind if I gave you a gift?"

He looked hopeful. "A gift?"

I smiled. "Yes," I said. "Would you like a nice new unibrow?"

The little beaver grinned so wide, it made me giggle.

"That would be ever so helpful," he replied.

"Done." With a wiggle of my fingers, Bob now had an impressive and hairy unibrow. He was thrilled. "Umm… Bob?"

"Yes?"

"How did Mae Blockinschlokinberg know our names?" I asked.

"She's a genius," Bob said, clearly having drunk the Mae Blockinschlokinbitch Kool-aid.

"Right." I glanced over at Zach who seemed perplexed as well.

"Willow, thank you so much for the unibrow. It's my pride and joy. I look forward to working together." He nodded his thanks and hustled off to continue writing.

"That was a very good question," Zach said.

I arched my brow. "Which one?"

"How *does* she know our names?"

"She's probably a mindreading heinous bitch cow," Sassy said, zooming by on her broom.

"Possibly," I agreed. The heinous bitch cow part was definitely accurate.

"Are we really going to do this?" Zach asked, still trying to figure out how we'd gotten ourselves buried in the shitstorm.

"I don't know how to act," I said, hoping it was an out.

"No worries," Sassy said, still zipping around the huge room on her broom. "I'm fabulous. I'll teach you everything you need to know! Just follow my lead."

"Well, that's certainly frightening," Zach muttered with a chuckle.

"Understatement," I whispered back with a grin.

Zorro walked over and gave us an adorable grin. "I think you should do it," he said, looking back and forth between Zach and me. "It will be the Three Musketeers back together again..."

"Four Musketeers," Sassy corrected Zorro as she flew past us upside down.

He shook his head at her. "It will be a gender-bending nightmare that will save the reputation of the Assjacket Community Theatre."

"Or kill it dead forever." I winced. "I don't think…" I began only to be cut off by Zach.

"We're in." He grabbed my hand and held it tight.

Trying to pull away was impossible. His grip was as strong as his sister's. And to be honest, I didn't want to pull away. I knew it would only prolong my heartache when I left, but it felt so right.

"Perfect," Roger the rabbit said, approaching us with a hop in his step. "Do any of you sing?"

"I do," Sassy yelled as she narrowly missed strafing the heads of all the Assjackians in the room.

Roger paled and his nose twitched in horror. "I ask again," he whispered. "Can any of you sing?"

"I shouldn't," I replied.

"Not a note," Zach added.

"Not well," Zorro said. "However, I'm excellent at talk-singing and bleating."

"Not to worry," Sassy squealed. "I'll sing for everyone. I'll switch languages for the different characters. Roger, just make sure none of the lyrics are Canadian. I don't speak that language."

Roger looked like he wanted to pass out. "Do any of you have a special talent?"

"Umm… I can lift heavy stuff, heal people and blow shit up," Zach offered as Roger nodded unenthusiastically.

"I speak Puntreelish," I said, watching Roger pale further.

"I pole dance," Zorro announced with pride. "And I can do the splits on the left side if that helps."

"It doesn't," Roger said. "But I will make it work."

The rabbit wandered off in a daze.

"I'm going to speak with DeeDee and Wanda," Zorro said, giving Zach and me quick hugs. "You'll love them. DeeDee's a deer Shifter and Wanda's a raccoon Shifter. They are costuming the show, and I want to get their approval on my assless chaps!"

I was frozen in my spot and prayed to the Goddess that I wasn't going to be wearing assless chaps while playing the sheriff as a man. Today had gone from weird to unbelievable.

Today couldn't get any stranger.

Or could it?

"Come with me," Zach said as he took my hand. "We have to talk."

Weird to unbelievable to stomach-churning. But I agreed with Zach.

We definitely needed to talk.

CHAPTER SIX

"Umm... Assjacket seems like a nice town," I said, searching for something to say to break the wildly uncomfortable awkwardness.

The town of Assjacket, West Virginia was located in the middle of nowhere and consisted of Main Street. The town square was dominated by a statue of a cement bear missing one side of his head. The rest of the block included a barbershop, hardware store, gas station and a mom and pop grocery along with a few other nondescript buildings.

We'd been walking in silence for fifteen minutes. Zach's grip had finally relaxed, so I removed my hand from his. Touching him felt lovely, but it was something I didn't want to get used to.

Zach nodded but said nothing.

I tried again. "Zelda's babies are adorable."

Again, he nodded. The warlock was so lost in his own thoughts, I didn't think he'd heard a word I'd said. I was starting to get annoyed. Zach had said he wanted to *talk*. This was a shitty talk.

Testing my theory, I tried one last time. "I lost my meat clackers somewhere along the way in life. My new wooden pappy, Sponge Bob, says I should go out into the world and search for my hairy magical beans. I'm going to wear spandex and channel Mick Jagger while I hunt down my nards."

"That's nice," Zach said with an absent nod of his head.

"Oh my Goddess! Did you hear a single word that came out of my mouth?" I demanded, squinting at him. He looked dumbstruck. Crap. Maybe he'd suffered brain damage from Henrietta Smith's attack. Immediately, I felt horrible for yelling at him.

Zach inhaled shakily. "I'm sorry," he said. "I need to tell you something, and I'm getting my courage up."

That didn't sound good. My stomach cramped, and I wanted to be anywhere else. He couldn't have missed that I'd been wildly in love with him for ten years. It had been embarrassingly obvious. Zach didn't feel the same way I did. That had been obvious, as well. I was fairly sure that he was about to let me down gently. Why hadn't I stayed in Sponge Bob's trunk? The real world was filled with heartbreak and humiliation.

Fine. This would definitely give me the closure I needed. It was time to roll and find my stones. Plastering a smile on my lips that I prayed didn't look as fake as it felt, I patted his back. "We're friends," I said. "You can tell me anything. That's what friends are for."

"But I don't want to be friends," Zach blurted out as I

gasped in complete shock and tripped over absolutely nothing. Before the pain of his words could overwhelm me, he added, "I mean, of course, I want to be your friend. Shit, I'm getting this all wrong."

"Just say it. It's better if you make it quick." I braced my heart. "Like ripping off a bandaid." Although, I feared it would be more like ripping duct tape off a hairy leg. I was sure what he had to say to me was going to hurt like hell and would most certainly leave a mark.

"You're right," Zach said, as he came to a jarring halt. "I'm in love with you, Willow."

My knees buckled and I landed in a heap on the sidewalk. I stared at the ground and tried to figure out how to respond. How could Zach be so mean? If he was making fun of me and my feelings for him, it would be devastating. My emotions ran amuck inside me, and I was at a loss for words, unsure if I was about to laugh, scream or cry. I looked around to see if we had witnesses. I sighed in relief that Main Street was empty.

Zelda had already explained that the town had been glamoured to look like a total dump on the outside so humans wouldn't want to stop. But inside the ramshackle structures, everything was pure enchantment. Shifters, witches and other magical beings lived very public but secret lives. A place like Assjacket was a perfect way to exist while hiding in plain sight.

Although, right now, I just wanted to hide *out* of plain sight.

"Wasn't exactly the reaction I was hoping for," Zach said as he gently helped me to my feet and made sure I was fine.

Narrowing my eyes, I punched him in the stomach. Hard. Just like his abs. "That was mean and uncalled for," I shouted.

Zach was wildly confused and completely unfazed by the punch. "It was?"

"Yes," I said, stomping away and sitting down on a cement bench beneath the half-headed bear. "It wasn't funny. I think you should apologize right now. Playing with other people is beneath you."

Zach followed me over to the bench and squatted down until he was eye level with me. Having him so close was killing me. My insides roiled with so many emotions I had no clue what to feel.

"I'm not playing with you, Willow," he said, staring so intensely into my eyes, I had to remind myself to breathe. "Until now, I had nothing to offer you. Nothing. The curse and the woman whose name I refuse to speak, tied me to a hell that I believed was permanent. I still don't have much to offer, but I can't hold back my feelings anymore. I don't want to. It's okay if you don't feel the same way anymore. I've probably killed anything you may have felt for me in the past. But I wanted you to know that I love you. I always have and always will."

His words were what I'd longed to hear for a decade, but...

"I loved you for so long," I whispered.

"Loved?" he questioned. "Past tense?"

"No. Yes. I don't know," I said. Zelda's words rang in my head. *You can't love someone until you love yourself.* Could

Zach truly love me if he still hated himself? Would my heart end up broken beyond repair?

Zach sat down next to me and offered his hand. He held his breath and waited. His pain was so evident, and so was his intent. He'd made his confession, and now the choice was mine.

I made it with my heart not my head. Slowly, I placed my hand in his. Our connection sent a tingle up my arm, and my head wreath twinkled and glowed. Zach's beautiful features relaxed as he closed his eyes for a moment.

"I despised myself," he said softly. "Bringing you into my hell by telling you how I truly felt was something I could never do. It would have been a fate worse than death for you. The fact that you stayed humbled me and consumed me with guilt."

"You knew I loved you?" I asked.

He nodded slowly. "It was the only thing that kept the agony at bay. It was incredibly selfish of me not to make both you and Zorro leave, but you and he were the only pure and beautiful things in my wretched existence."

"Neither of us would have ever left you," I said as my heart hurt for him… and Zorro and me.

It had been a decade of sadness and tremendous pain. However, I wouldn't have traded it for the world. There had been beautiful times too. Leaving Zach completely alone with that horrible murderous woman would have been unacceptable. Zorro had felt the same.

"I know you wouldn't have left," he said tightly. "It's one of the many reasons I wouldn't leave you."

"What do you mean?"

"You almost *died*, Willow. If Zelda hadn't gotten you to Sponge Bob in time, I think I would have died with you." He shook his head and pressed his temples. "Zorro held me together. I spent every day and all night in the grove under the mighty oaks, sometimes to the point where I'd forget to eat, to sleep. Zorro made sure I did both with very colorful and persuasive language… and one sound kick to my ass."

I smiled. "He is a bit bossy." How many times had Zorro been there for Zach and me over the past decade? Goddess, he must have been as scared as Zach, but he kept his focus on hope and not despair. Zorro embodied hope.

"I can't imagine my life without you in it even though you deserve more." I could see the struggle within him as he clenched his jaw. "Sometimes, it makes me detest myself even more."

I sighed and longed to lean into Zach, but didn't. Self-preservation instincts weren't my forte, but I was developing them. My hairy magical beans were finally emerging.

"This is a lot to take in," I whispered, unsure how to proceed.

"I know," he replied, running his hands through his hair in frustration. "It's probably as selfish as anything I've ever done. If I wasn't a self-serving bastard, I would have kept my mouth shut."

"No," I said, wanting him to understand. "No, to hear you say the words is what I've dreamed of for years, but … but I don't know *how* to believe you even though I want to. I'm terrified."

The conversation wasn't even close to what I'd dreamt

this moment might be, but *reali-tree* was stranger than fiction by a long shot.

Zach took in what I said and was silent for a few moments. His handsome face darkened with sadness then a very small smile began to tug at his lips. His green eyes sparkled and my heart skipped a beat. "Will you let me prove it, Willow? Give me a chance? I'm still not sure I'm worth the risk, but I..."

Placing my finger over the lips I wanted to kiss, I shushed him. His feelings of worthlessness were going to be a problem.

What I really wanted to do was throw myself into his arms, ignore all the uncertainties of our past that we should discuss, and live happily ever after. However, that was a recipe for disaster. Our reality had been a disaster for so long, I wasn't sure how to handle the possibility of a new one. But...

"I have a thought," I told him, thinking I might be insane. "It's a little crazy."

"Like Sassy crazy?"

"Yep," I said. "Although, it's more a suggestion than a thought."

"Will you be speaking Canadian?" he inquired with a charming lopsided grin that made me giggle.

There were so many reasons I'd fallen in love with the broken man sitting next to me. His goodness through his despicable situation was always there. He'd rescued Zorro when his pack had left him for dead. He'd welcomed me, an orphaned, lonely dryad without question. We became a pack of misfits. No matter how weak or drained of blood and magic he was, he'd sheltered both Zorro and I. And in turn, we'd sheltered him as much as we could.

His compassion had almost killed him, but his sense of humor had remained intact. His outer beauty didn't compare to his inner beauty, but he had no clue. That was part of the issue.

"Yes, I will be speaking purely in Canadian. Do you understand it?" I asked.

"Actually, I do," he replied. "I even understand and speak a little Puntreelish, dryad."

"Interesting, warlock," I said, raising a brow. "Shall we test that claim out?"

"*Absolu-tree*," Zach said, mirroring my raised brow.

"What did the mighty oak wear to the pool party?" I asked.

"Swimming trunks," he replied with a chuckle.

"Okay, you got one," I conceded with a smile, loving the carefree lightness in his voice. "Could have been a lucky guess. What did Luke Skywalker say to the tree?"

Without missing a beat, Zach answered. "May the forest be with you."

I laughed and was delighted. Hmm… I wanted to *stump* him. "What did the single tree say to the bush?"

"Easy," Zach replied, looking cocky and pleased. "I don't want no shrub. A shrub is a guy who can't get no love from me."

I grinned so wide, it hurt my cheeks.

Zach went for it. "Willow, I don't deserve you. I'm very aware of that, but I would do anything for a chance. We could date. We could start at the beginning. We could get to know each other."

He was so wrong about not deserving me, but I knew he wouldn't believe me if I told him.

"Anything?" I asked, forming a plan in my head. "You would do anything?"

"Yes," Zach said without hesitation. "Anything."

"Would you do couples therapy with me?" I questioned.

Zach looked surprised, but quickly nodded. "Yes. Is there a therapist in Assjacket?"

I nodded. "Roger is a therapist. As a matter of fact, he's Zelda's therapist."

"The rabbit who was making up songs about graphically getting eaten by sharks?" Zach asked, worried.

"Yep," I replied with a laugh. "And he apparently enjoys porn."

"You think that's a good idea?" he asked, skeptically. "Zelda's not exactly a stable individual as far as therapy success stories go."

"Your sister is wonderful," I insisted. "You know it as well as I do."

Zach looked down and grinned. "Yes, my *sister* is wonderful," he admitted. "I'm still getting used to the word sister."

"And I'm getting used to the words you started this conversation with," I said, feeling lighter than I had in a very long time.

He gazed at me. The sincerity in his gorgeous green eyes was unmistakable. "Will it take you long to believe me?" he asked.

"That depends on you... and me," I answered truthfully. Although, if it was up to my girlie parts, the process wouldn't take long at all.

Zach laced his fingers in mine. Our connection made my wreath glow and sparkle. He touched one of the flowers with reverence and smiled.

"I'll do whatever it takes," he promised.

My heart pounded a wild happy beat in my chest. Pure and simple. And it was all I could do not to climb up Zach's trunk and shake his leaves until we were one. But I knew that sex would complicate everything. While my body disagreed vehemently, I let my brain take the wheel. I wanted Zach forever, not just right now. But first... "Can you learn to love yourself?"

His fingers tightened on mine. "Shit," he muttered, looking bewildered. "Is that a requirement?"

"It is," I said softly.

Zach's expression turned wary and pained. His fingers slid out of mine. "It's something I've never done," he admitted.

I wanted to hold Zach tight and tell him it would be all right, but his healing process was up to him. "I think there are a few people here who would be happy to help."

Zach sighed and ran his hands through his hair. It stuck straight up on his head. He looked so much like Fabio it was striking. His lips compressed and his jaw worked a mile a minute. I could almost hear the chaotic shouting match in his mind. I was asking him to undo a lifetime of hurt and self-hatred.

It was not a small request, but it was the only way to

make it work. And even if *we* didn't work, I would be happy if he could love himself and find real happiness.

"I can try," Zach said, slowly. "I can't guarantee success, but if it means I'll be worthy of you, I promise to try."

He needed to do it for himself, but we'd get to that—one magical baby step at a time.

CHAPTER SEVEN

"I WILL BREAK YOU DOWN TO NOTHING AND REMOLD YOU IN my image, you lowly pieces of talentless crap," Mae Blockin-schlokinberg screamed in an octave that should have attracted stray dogs from hundreds of miles away.

She clearly hadn't looked in a mirror during the break. The bushy beige unibrow was still front and center on her forehead. Her buddies sucked in the friend department. Friends told friends if they were sporting a unibrow.

Rehearsal wasn't going well. The icky little block of a woman paced the back of the hall and barked orders at Bob while slinging profanities and insults at everyone. Her ghastly dressed minions sat in the back row and said nothing. Although, they clapped wildly and took pictures each time she pointed at them. Honestly, I was only half paying attention. Every time I glanced over at Zach, he was staring right back at me with a huge grin on his face. His words from earlier still danced in my brain.

The situation we were currently in was hellish, but the company—excluding Mae Blockinschlokinberg and her sandal-wearing posse—was divine.

"Holy shit," Sassy muttered. "I'd rather be human than look like her. If this fucking play didn't mean so much to Bob and the reputation of Assjacket, I'd wax that noxious turd so fast she wouldn't even see me coming. That's Japanese for dehairing a gaping thunder hole."

"Are you sure that was Japanese, guurrlfriend?" Zorro asked with a chuckle. He sat in a kiddie pool he'd acquired during the break in order to find his inner-shark wearing his pink assless chaps.

"Might have been Canadian," Sassy conceded, giggling.

In the short time we'd been at it, Bob had already removed half of his new unibrow as he wrote and rewrote the script according to Mae Blockinschlokinberg's bizarre and offensive visions. Zorro splashed around in six inches of water and gnashed his teeth like a shark. When Zach wasn't smiling at me, he looked like he wanted to tear Mae Blockinschlokinberg's head from her squishy shoulders, and Roger continued to plunk out songs about massive teeth biting tasty bottoms. If it wasn't my *reali-tree*, I would have laughed.

"You. Dryad," Mae Blockinschlokinberg shouted at me. "You're dreadful. I want you to get bitten by the shark in the pink pants then do an interpretive dance about death and sharp teeth embedded in your ass. Everyone else do deep knee bends and grunt. The ensemble will represent the blood and innards of the victim. Make sure your grunts sound like kidneys and bowels."

"Seriously?" I asked, sucking my bottom lip into my mouth so I didn't call her a gaping jackhole. The strange and uncomfortable sensations I'd felt earlier returned. I tried to shake them, but the more she focused her putrid attention on me, the more they intensified.

"Do I sound like I'm joking?" she demanded.

"You sound like you're missing a few screws," I muttered under my breath. Goddess, how I loathed this woman.

"I'll do it," Sassy said, saving me from the humiliation. "I'm excellent with interpretive death dances. It's one of my foreplay moves with my mate Jeeves. Zorro, bite my butt—not really hard, but make it look good. I'll scream and shimmy a little. Also, I'll roll my head so my hair will be featured since it's fabulous and blonde. I'm going for a tragic yet really hot vibe. Roger, you sing the part about the bloody detached fingers and the fact that we're destroying the oceans with prophylactics like condoms."

"Umm… it's plastics—*not prophylactics*," Roger corrected her.

"Whoops, my bad," Sassy said as she stretched a bit to warm up for her dance. "I must have misunderstood because I was thinking in British and you were speaking French. Happens all the time."

Amazingly, Sassy was even able to render Mae Blockinschlokinberg silent. Sassy was a very powerful weapon of mass confusion.

"Hit it," she shouted as she stuck out her bottom for Zorro to bite. The next fifteen minutes defied logic. Sassy gyrated. Zorro gnashed. Roger sang. Zach and I grunted, searching desperately for a noise that sounded like a kidney or a bowel.

As Roger warbled about bloody appendages in an up-tempo jazzy beat, Zorro hopped out of the kiddie pool and darted to the wings. He dragged out a glittering pink pole that he'd clearly stashed as a just in case prop. Straddling the pole, he did a routine that would have made the Goddess blush. Sassy, not to be outdone by her fabulous, bare-assed goat co-star, grabbed her broom and made it an obscene duet.

Roger's visually disgusting lyrics punctuated by laughing grunts from Zach and me created a shitshow like no other. It was mortifying, hilarious and so very wrong. However, the crowning jewel was when Sassy waved her hands and dressed all of us in matching pink ass-less leather chaps.

"Nope," Zach yelled, falling over and laughing. "I'm done."

"Oh my Goddess," I said, looking over my shoulder at my bare butt. "I don't think the sheriff would wear something with his ass hanging out."

"However, the ass is outstanding," Zach commented as I blushed furiously.

Sassy bounced over and grinned. "I don't need to send the note," she told me. "He definitely likes you."

Waving my hand, I replaced my obscene pants with a rocking Prada mini dress. "Yep. He likes me. No need for the note."

"I'm just so excited he's not a hermaphrodite," she said, hopping onto her broom and flying in tiny circles around the kiddie pool.

"AND CUT. I'm BRILLIANT," Mae Blockinschlokinberg yelled as her followers applauded with gusto. "That was perfect. Bob, did you get all of that down?"

"For real?" Bob choked out, yanking at the few hairs left in his unibrow.

I was going to have to supply Bob with many unibrows over the next week. He was plucking them off as fast as I was putting them back on.

"Yesssssssss, for real," Mae Blockinschlokinberg snarled. "What we just observed was utter brilliance from my unparalleled prowess. Nothing like this has ever been performed. It's genius because of *me*. I shall be the toast of the community theatre world. I'll be back tomorrow. We will add the orgy and the grisly death of the sheriff. And fire the costumers. The show shall be done in the nude."

"What the fuck?" Zach muttered, shaking his head and squinting at all of us in shock.

"Hang on a sec. I'd like to call a quick cast meeting," I insisted as Mae Blockinschlokinberg stared daggers at me.

"I second that," Zach said, backing me up.

"And I third it," Bob added in a defeated tone.

Bob, Roger, Zorro, Sassy, Zach and I huddled together on the stage out of earshot of the insane woman.

"What's wrong?" Sassy whispered.

"Everything, guurrlfriend," Zorro said with a chuckle. "While I have no problem sharing my fine tushy with the world. Not sure displaying my Johnson is a good plan in my newly adopted town."

Roger's nose twitched and he wrung his hands. "I'm

afraid Zorro is correct. Swinging Johnsons and bouncing bosoms don't really scream family-friendly show."

The crazed clicking and flashing of phone cameras made me glance to the back of the room.

"Do her minions ever speak?" I asked, watching the little horrors point and take pictures of us while Mae Blockinschlokinberg paced the back of the hall, looking like a bomb about to go off.

"Haven't heard them utter a word," Roger said with a shudder.

"They probably speak Nard-Hole-ish," Sassy informed us, nodding her head seriously. "It's the language of asspipes who have no fashion sense and are addicted to their phones."

There was a moment of silence after Sassy's revelation... or it was possible we needed a few seconds to bite back our laughter. Sassy was a font of nonsense, and I liked her more with each bizarre fact.

"I need a clarification," Bob said, getting back to the matter at hand. "Is there an orgy in *Jaws*?"

"Not that I recall," Roger volunteered, scratching his head in confusion.

"No, guurrlfriends and boyfriends," Zorro said. "There was *no* orgy in *Jaws*."

"And I die a grisly death?" I questioned. "In the movie, Roy Scheider lives."

"I can't do this," Zach said, snapping his fingers and replacing his assless pink chaps with a pair of faded jeans that made my mouth water. "Actually, none of us should do this. We will *never* live this down."

"As much as I want to win an award, I have to agree," Bob said sadly.

Roger shook his head and bounced on his toes. "I concur. We will have to take the financial hit and the insufferable gloating from the Tennessee Man-Titty Thespians. It will be a bitter pill to swallow, but maybe a few years from now, we can redeem our heartbreaking and humiliating failure. We must fire Mae Blockinschlokinberg."

Bob pulled a plastic baggy of berries from his pocket and swallowed them back like they were antacids. Waving my hand, I supplied everyone with nose plugs. I had no problem with Bob needing his magical berries, I simply didn't want the stage covered in vomit when he started tooting. We had enough of a mess to deal with as it was.

"I'll make up the financial loss," Zach said before I could volunteer. "I would be delighted to cough up my savings to get out of this. How much did you pay Mae Blockinschlokinberg?"

"Two hundred thousand dollars," Bob whispered, starting to cry as he kept cramming berries into his mouth. "Our investor is likely to be *very* upset."

"Understatement," Roger agreed with agitation.

"Wow," I muttered, thinking my twenty thousand in the bank wouldn't even help much. Any time I'd needed money over the years, I'd taught botany in magical schools. As a dryad, it fit my skillset *perfec-tree-ly*. I'd have to *log* a heck of a lot of hours in the classroom to help Bob and Roger out. "That's a lot of money."

Zorro fainted.

"I can't cover that," Zach said as surprised as I was by the amount.

"Holy shee-ot," Zorro added as he came to and got back to his feet. "That's a lot of hay." He gave a low whistle. "Where did you people get that kind of money for a community theatre? What kind of high falootin' investor do you Shifters have?"

Bob leaned in and his eyes grew huge. "Cats," he whispered. He farted, and the magical berry gas gagged us all.

Quickly, everyone put on their nose plugs. Bob grimaced in apology.

"Your investors are *cats*?" I asked a bit nasally since my nose was now plugged. I wasn't positive I'd heard him correctly.

"Not exactly, but the wise guy cats represent our super-secret investor. We have no clue who the money man actually is," Roger said, glancing around warily. "But from what we understand, he wants a return on his investment, or we'll be put in cement shoes and thrown in the Assjacket river."

Zach's eyes narrowed. I could tell he was trying not to laugh. "Names. Give me the names of the wise guy cats."

Again, Roger glanced around. Bob removed the last two strands of his unibrow. He looked to Roger who gave him a curt nod.

"Fat Bastard, Jango Fett and Boba Fett," Bob revealed with a gulp.

It was my turn to try not to laugh. How on the Goddess's green earth did Zelda's cats get involved with someone who had that kind of money?

"My sister's *familiars* are the wise guy cats representing your illustrious investor?" Zach asked, squinting at Roger and Bob in amusement.

Sassy smacked her forehead and giggled. "I can't believe it, but I have an excellent idea," she announced. "I'll wax the cats and get the name of the investor."

"Or," I suggested quickly before anyone agreed to her awful plan. "I can ask them. They owe me a favor for de-stinking them. We should start at the point of least destruction and retribution."

Sassy cocked her head to the side in curiosity. "Was that German?"

"Umm… yes," I said to save time.

There was no way I was going to grunt on stage naked then go through a grisly death. It was also abundantly clear that it would be devastating for Bob and Roger to lose their reputation in the community theatre world and possibly their lives to the *investor*. But Mae Blockinschlokinberg had to go. We'd work the rest out later.

The cats did owe me a favor, and it would be a good way to use it. Maybe, I could get the hairy feline boys to give me the name of the investor. Maybe, the investor would listen to reason or at the very least, accept a payment plan. If we pooled our money together, and I found a teaching job, we could make it work. Saving people's lives and avoiding public humiliation was a fine plan. Worst case scenario, we performed the nightmare-inducing play minus the director.

"It might be dangerous," Bob said to me.

"It will be fine," I promised, hoping I was right.

Roger nodded his agreement. "Willow has big balls. And

I'd like to offer up a few free therapy sessions as a gift to you."

I was thrilled that so many people thought I had hairy magical beans. I knew they were incorrect, but it was encouraging. And Roger's offer had come at the perfect time.

"Would you be willing to do couples therapy?" I asked, glancing over at Zach who gave me a thumbs up.

"*Absolu-tree*," Roger said with a wink. "I know a little Puntreelish!"

Bob glanced back at Mae Blockinschlokinberg and squeaked in terror. "Okay, we need to make a move. It looks like that woman wants to eat all of us. Who's going to do it?"

"I'd be overjoyed to fire her," Zach insisted much to the relief of Roger and Bob. "*Nothing* would give me more pleasure."

"Will she retaliate?" I asked, wondering how the nasty little woman would react.

"She's got her money," Bob said, sounding worried about the prospect of a counterattack by the abomination. "There's no breach in contract. We have fulfilled our end."

"Now, we just have to worry about the investor," Roger said, paling considerably and looking like he might join Zorro's club and faint.

I wasn't sure if it was Bob's gas or the thought of cement shoes. Possibly both.

This town was wonderful in every odd and strange little way. I loved it here. Now, all we had to do was fire Mae Blockinschlokinberg and cut a deal with the investor so no one died and it would be perfect.

"We ready?" Zach asked with a wide grin.

"Yep," I said, taking in the relieved and terrified nods of the group.

"Hey, Mae Blockinschlokinberg," Zach said, walking to the edge of the stage. "You're fired."

Mae Blockinschlokinberg turned purple and began to hiss furiously. Her minions dropped to the ground and began throwing tantrums that would have made a two-year-old hopped up on ten pounds of sugar proud. It was disturbing and bizarre. Mae Blockinschlokinberg waved her hands and a foul scented gray wind blew through the room. I winced and gagged. It was so putrid I could smell it even through the nose plug.

"What did you say, you worthless piece of crap?" she bellowed at Zach as a slimy film covered her face and dripped off of her beige unibrow.

"Umm... she's not taking it very well," Sassy said, waving her hand in front of her nose frantically. "I think she might have eaten an assload of Bob's magical stank berries."

"You're fired," Zach repeated with a grin on his face.

"I do NOT accept," she shrieked. "No one has ever fired me and *no one* ever will who wants to live to tell."

"There's a first time for everything, lady—and I use the term lightly," I said, doing my best to stay diplomatic even though all I wanted to do was blast the awful woman and her posse right out of Assjacket. I wasn't letting Zach take all the heat, even though he seemed to be enjoying it.

"I have an iron-clad contract. I am un-terminatable," she snarled as her beady eyes bulged beneath her slime-covered beige unibrow. "I'll be back... tomorrow, and we will

89

continue with the sheriff's death scene and the orgy blood-
bath or you will *regret* it. I can promise you that."

With her horrifying refusal to be fired, Mae Blockinschlokinberg and her entourage waddled quickly out of the
building.

"Can she do that?" Sassy asked, confused.

"She just did," Zorro pointed out with a laugh of
disbelief.

"That was total bullshit," Zach said. "Is she correct about
her contract? Is it iron-clad against her firing?"

Bob began to cry again. "I don't know," he blubbered.
"She sent us a four hundred and forty-two-page contract
and insisted we sign immediately."

"Did you read it?" I asked as my stomach churned.

Bob and Roger both shook their heads no.

"I tried," Bob admitted. "But it all looked like Latin to
me. Besides, she's not the kind of woman you keep waiting."
Bob tooted then gasped in embarrassment. "So sorry," he
apologized sincerely. However, the smelly effect of his
snack choice didn't stop him from cramming more berries
into his mouth.

Crap. We couldn't fire her? This was an unexpected
wrinkle.

"And you signed the contract?" I pressed.

Again, the boys nodded.

Double crap. They were already out two hundred
thousand dollars to an investor who wanted a return on
his money. If Mae Blockinschlokinberg sued over
wrongful firing, there was no telling how much that
would cost.

Roger hopped around the stage. Bob pulled out a second bag of berries and went to town on them.

"Here's what we'll do," Roger said, mulling it aloud as he worked out the particulars. "Until we find the investor and cut a repayment deal, we pretend we're still doing the show. We'll show up at rehearsal tomorrow and act as if everything is normal—normal being a relative word. In the meantime, I'll read the contract… which might have been helpful to do in the first place."

"Is it in French?" Sassy asked. "Because if it is, I can help."

Roger's laughed. "No, but thank you for the offer, my dear. You're a very good witch."

Sassy was elated by the praise. She hopped back on her broom and whipped around the large hall. "No worries. If you get stuck, just let me know. I speak at least fifty-seven languages."

"Will do," Roger replied.

"Alrighty then," I said, looking at each member of our little group. "Roger, read the contract. See if Mae Blockin-schlokinberg is bluffing. Bob, cut back on the berries. The paint is starting to peel off the walls. I'm going to get the investor's name from the cats then plead our case so no one has to wear cement shoes."

"*We* are going to find the cats and have a chat with the investor. I'm your partner in this venture," Zach said, taking my hand in his.

"And I'm your backup," Zorro added, taking my other hand.

"And I will fly you guys on my broom back to Zelda's place," Sassy said.

"NO," we all shouted in horror at the same time.

"We'll walk," I said quickly. "I need the exercise after living in a tree for a month."

Sassy shrugged and saluted us. "Suit yourselves. I'll meet you there."

CHAPTER EIGHT

"WELL, THAT WAS CERTAINLY A SHITSHOW," ZORRO SAID, walking with Zach and me down the road that led to Zelda and Mac's house.

"Understatement," Zach said. "However, if we want to look at the bright side, we're no longer living in the clutches of a voodoo witch who drank our blood and depleted our magic to stay young. I still say it's a win."

"While I'd definitely have to qualify the naked musical version of *Jaws* as a living nightmare, I'm going to agree with Zach," I stated, walking between my two favorite men. "We're in a much better place now. Period."

"Guurrlfriend, ain't that the truth," Zorro concurred then observed us with amused and delighted curiosity. "Whoopsy-doodle, I left my man purse back at the community center. I'm just gonna zip back and grab it. Y'all go ahead and I'll meet up with you back at the ranch."

I eyed Zorro silently. He grinned, winked, and sprinted off in a flash.

Zach raised a brow. "He didn't bring his man purse to the theatre."

"Nope, he did not," I said, feeling shy all of a sudden. "I think he noticed… umm… us."

"Is there an us?" he asked hopefully, searching my eyes for an answer.

"There's a beginning of an *us*," I said with a smile. "We're taking baby steps right now."

"I know we have a lot on our plate at the moment," Zach said. "But let's start our baby steps on this walk—our unofficial first date. No talk of Mae Blockinschlokinberg, investors or grunting like a kidney while naked."

"Works for me," I told him with a thumbs up. "I'd be fine never saying the words naked, grunting, or kidney in the same sentence for the rest of my life."

Zach chuckled and shortened his stride to match mine. "What's your favorite color?" he asked.

"For real?" I shot back, wrinkling my nose at him.

"Yes, for real," he said, grinning. "We're starting from the beginning—baby steps."

"And you don't know my favorite color?" I pressed.

"I do," he admitted sheepishly. "I've just never heard it from your mouth."

I rolled my eyes and played along. "Green."

"For the trees?" he asked.

"Yes, and your eyes," I blabbed before I could stop the words from leaving my lips.

His grin grew wider. Mine did as well, along with my

embarrassment. Whatever. I wasn't about to lie now. It would be a ridiculous waste of time.

"And yours?" I asked.

His gaze locked with mine. "Same," he replied.

"That's cheating," I told him.

"Not cheating if it's true."

Again, I rolled my eyes. "My turn. Umm… holiday. What's your favorite holiday?" I asked and then wanted to punch myself in the head.

There had been no holidays in his life. No parties. No presents. No cakes. No mother or father who loved him… although, Zach did have a father who wanted to love him now, he just didn't want anything to do with Fabio.

But that was a discussion for another time.

Zach's face fell for the briefest of seconds, but he recovered quickly. "I have no idea," he said, taking my hand and pulling me along the trail. "And it's okay to ask. I'll choose Halloween, even though I've never trick-or-treated."

"Maybe we can take Zelda's toddlers trick-or-treating in October," I suggested, still feeling like a dummy for asking a painful question. "It might be kind of weird if we went without kids in tow."

"It's a date," he said with a smile that lit his face. "Means you have to stick around for a few months, and I get more time to win you."

The man had already won me. He just needed to win himself.

"Deal," I said with a giggle.

"You've been in my life for ten years, forty-four days, and eight hours. I was alive for a few decades before we

95

met," Zach said, trying to make me feel better about my query. "I could have celebrated a holiday before you knew me."

That was not true. He knew it and I knew it. But wait…

My mouth hung open. "How many seconds have I been in your life?" I asked, shocked that he'd kept track. It was so freaking romantic.

Looking down at his watch, he calculated. "Twenty-three," he replied.

"Holy cow," I muttered. "*That* is impressive."

"I'm an impressive warlock," he said with a smirk. "I also remember what you wore the first time I saw you."

"I don't even remember what I was wearing," I said, trying to recall.

"Obviously it was green," he said with a laugh then grew very serious. "It was a green dress with tiny gold flowers all over it. It was torn at the sleeve, and you were bleeding. The wreath on your head was wilted and your eyes were filled with tears. But then you smiled at me and my world tilted on its axis. Your smile was the most beautiful thing I'd ever seen. I fell for you in that moment."

I tugged him to a stop. My eyes welled up. I remembered the moment too. It was seared into my mind. My world had tilted on its axis as well the first time I'd seen him. I'd been lost and searching for so long. Being alone in the forest for so many decades, I was almost wild. Zach's beauty and kindness anchored me in reality. Zorro was the added bonus. Zorro was hope and Zach was the man I'd always dreamed about. They had given me a home and refused to give up on me even when I wanted to run or self-destruct. It was why I would never ever give up on either of them.

"Zach, we wasted so much time," I whispered.

Turning away from me, he ran his hands through his hair and shook his head angrily. "No. We didn't. Willow, I was nothing. I had nothing to give anyone. Goddess knows, I'm still not good enough for you."

"You've always been good enough for me," I insisted truthfully, carefully touching his rigid back. "You loved me in the only way you could and knew that I loved you in return. However, one piece of the puzzle is still missing."

"One?" he asked hollowly. "I'd say many pieces."

"No, just one. You could never fully love me," I said.

"I loved you with all I had to give... which sadly wasn't much," he said tightly, still facing away from me. "It was pathetic compared to what you gave to me."

"You can never love anyone else completely until you love yourself," I said quietly.

"I know..." Zach's body jerked and sparks began to fly from his fingertips. "Goddess, we might be doomed, Willow," he said, sounding devastated. "It's impossible for me to see a day when I can say I love myself. I've done too many horrible things."

He was so wrong.

"Impossible?" I asked.

"Improbable," he conceded, turning to meet my gaze. "I'm not worth it. I wish I was... but I don't know if I am. You should probably cut your losses and run."

"I'll be the judge of that," I said, touching his cheek and wanting to take the pain away.

But I couldn't. He had to make the decision to release it to begin to heal.

"No more twenty questions," I said, taking his hand firmly in mine. "Let's concentrate on right now—baby steps."

Zach sighed and squeezed my hand. The feeling was one I'd longed for. Our magic intertwined and a glittering shower of blue, green and golden sparkles rained down on us. "I'll have to deal with my past if I want to have you—all of you—in my future. You deserve someone who can truly love you."

"And I will have him," I said, smiling. "I believe the improbable is very possible."

"You're crazy," he said, cupping my face lovingly in his hands.

"Your point?"

"No point. Just a beautiful and wondrous observation," he replied.

I wanted to kiss him so badly, I could taste it. But the physical part could wait. When we finally came together—and I prayed to the Goddess that we would—there would be no barrier from the past between us.

"I'll wait for you," I promised.

"You've already waited a very long time," he said sadly.

"Good things come to those who wait," I said. "That was Canadian."

Zach threw his head back and laughed. "You make me so happy, Willow."

"Back at you," I replied, feeling tingly all over. "Shall we poof back to the house or do you want to walk."

"Walk," he replied, still looking a little sad and serious. "Being alone with you and holding your hand in mine is the best I've felt in my whole life so far."

"Better than when we were grunting kidneys and bowels?" I asked with a giggle.

I wanted to see him smile. He needed to smile and laugh more. Assjacket—as horribly named as it was—was a magical place. It was a happy place. Zach, Zorro and I needed this place. And we were blessed by the Goddess that it found us.

"Yes, far better than our grunting innards performance." Zach grinned. "Shall we?"

"Yes. We shall."

CHAPTER NINE

IT TOOK US A HALF HOUR TO REACH OUR DESTINATION AND each baby step was magical. I felt my head wreath blossom in a glittering array of colors. Shimmering pops of enchantment danced around us as we shared secrets and dreams. While I knew we had work ahead, I looked forward to it. I believed in Zach even if he didn't believe in himself yet. I was almost bummed when we'd finally arrived back at Zelda's, but there was a lifetime left to discover more about each other. Plus, we had a mission—an important one.

Strangely, walking up the stairs of Zelda's front porch with Zach's hand in mine felt like coming home. I waved to my tree family and they rustled with happiness.

I might not have located my hairy magical beans, but I'd found love. It was a little complicated, but nothing worth it was easy. I was sure Sponge Bob and the boys would be proud of me. And Zorro would be thrilled.

I'd half expected Zorro to beat us back to the house, but

when we arrived it was just Zelda, Mac and Sassy. And the intel was bizarre. Seriously bizarre.

"I'm sorry, what did you say?" I asked Mac, wondering if I needed to get my hearing checked.

Sassy had caught Zelda and Mac up on the shitshow that had gone down at the community theatre before Zach and I had arrived, so we just jumped right in. I would have loved to have heard her interpretation, but we had more important things to discuss. Life and death important.

"They're slugs," Mac said.

"Slugs? Mae Blockinschlokinberg and her cronies are *slugs*?" Zach asked with a scoff of disbelief. "You're shitting me."

"I shit you not, brother-in-law," Mac replied with a chuckle and a shake of his head. "Haven't come across a slug in a few decades, but they're definitely slugs."

Mac was Zelda's mate. He was a werewolf and the King of the Shifters, along with being the official sheriff of Assjacket, West Virginia. The werewolf was intimidating, yet fair and kind—not to mention, very handsome. He stood about the same height as Zach—six foot-four. Mac had bright blue eyes and an unmeasurable amount of love for Zelda and their babies.

"Seriously?" I asked, wrinkling my nose. "Slug Shifters exist?"

The unibrow slime certainly made more sense now.

"Yep," Mac replied with a slight shudder. "Rare and… umm… unusual. The five of them registered in town two days ago when they got here. Said they were staying a week for the show."

"Where are the *slugs* staying?" Zach asked, still absorbing the slimy news of Mae Blockinschlokinberg's species.

Who knew slug Shifters were a thing? Now I'd heard everything. I hoped.

"Outside of town somewhere in tents," Mac replied. "When it was determined that the Assjacket Diner didn't serve earthworms, bug-infested leaves or raw snails, they decided to shack up in the forest for the duration of their visit."

"Sounds about right," Sassy said, sitting on the ground playing with Audrey's dollhouse. "That would explain the old lady crouch smell."

"Did you just say old lady crouch?" I asked, bewildered.

"Yep," Sassy confirmed with a very serious expression. "You know—the smell when you go into the bathroom at the country club... powdery old lady crouch."

I was incredibly sorry I'd asked. So was everyone else in the room if the groans were any indication. "I won't be able to remove that from my brain," I muttered.

"Only a lobotomy can erase it," Sassy informed me. "I wouldn't recommend one."

"Got it," I said as I swore to myself I'd stop asking Sassy what she meant for the rest of my days.

"I am so fucking confused by the psycho-babble Sassy spewed before you guys got here," Zelda said, looking over at her mate, whose expression matched hers.

Mac shrugged and grinned. "Maybe Sassy was speaking *French*."

"It's a good guess, but I was speaking British," Sassy explained, busy rearranging a tiny bedroom in the dollhouse. "If you drink some tea, you'll understand me better."

Zelda rolled her eyes. "Most gaggingly important, is it true that this Mae Blockinschlokinberg slug-bitch from fashion hell was wearing black socks and beige sandals?"

"It is," I confirmed, gagging a little myself. "That was the nicest thing about her. She's horrid."

"And Bob is gunning for a *communist* theatre award?" Zelda asked, trying not to laugh.

"I'm going to go out on a limb and guess that the *communist* theatre award is Canadian for *community* theatre award," I said, walking over to the bay window and glancing out to see if Zorro was on his way. Maybe he'd run into Roger and Bob at the community center and stayed to chat. Zorro was a very popular person and with good reason. He was pure joy.

"Correct!" Sassy chimed in. "Sometimes, I get confused and speak in ten different languages in the same sentence. It's hard being as promiscuous as I am."

"I'm not touching that," Zelda muttered with an eye roll. "I want to *really* badly, but I'm not gonna."

Mac grinned. "That's very mature, babe."

"Being mature makes me itchy," she complained.

Mac kissed the top of Zelda's head then turned his attention back to us.

"Is it true that the slug has already been paid? In full?" Mac inquired.

"According to Roger and Bob, she has... to the tune of two hundred thousand dollars," Zach said. "And that's the real issue other than the minor fact that Mae Blockin-schlokinberg won't accept that she's fired."

Zelda squinted at Mac in surprise and he shrugged. "I've never known the Assjacket Community Theatre to have that kind of money," Mac said, perplexed.

"There's a super-secret blood-thirsty investor who's partial to cement shoes and the bottoms of rivers if he doesn't see a return on his investment. We need to talk to him and work out a payment plan so Roger and Bob don't get whacked," I told them. "Apparently, your cats know who it is."

Zelda twisted her hair in her fingers and frowned. "Those dumbass hairy ball-lickers are always involved with the shady side of Assjacket. And of course, they've conveniently disappeared. My guess is they're on a quest to find someone stupid enough to sniff their cracks. Are you *sure* Bob and Roger's lives are on the line?"

"Yep," I said, feeling a horrible sense of dread. The cats could be gone for a very long time if crack sniffing was their goal. "We have to find them now. Fat Bastard and the boys can lead us to the investor. If he hears Mae Blockin-schlokinberg has been fired, he might send his people to fit Bob and Roger for cement shoes."

"*No one* is going to wear cement shoes in my town," Mac growled and picked up his cellphone. "I'll put security on Bob and Roger immediately."

"Perfect," Zach said with a sigh of relief, watching Mac text in the order for protection.

"Do the cats have cellphones?" I asked and then laughed at the question. They didn't have hands or fingers so to speak. They had cute chubby toe beans. Why would they have cellphones?

Zelda grinned and shook her head. "Nope. I can call them back with a spell, but it could take a day or two depending on the magical connection and how far away they are," she said, checking the video baby monitor to make sure Henry and Audrey were still napping.

"Two days? You're kidding. That's not going to work," Zach said, running his hands through his hair in frustration. "We need to get started now. Plus, I can't be a grunting kidney or writhing bowel in assless chaps."

"And I can't die a grizzly death in pink assless chaps," I added.

"I'm not going to touch that either even though it's killing me," Zelda said, shaking her head sadly. "Let me call the furry menaces home. Zach, hold my hand. The spell will be more powerful."

Zach grabbed his sister's hands. Mac nodded at me to back away. I'd witnessed some of Zelda's spells. Mac's silent advice was excellent.

"You guys want my magic too?" Sassy inquired. "I can think in Spanish just in case the cats went to England."

Zelda closed her eyes, shook her head and laughed. "Sure," she said. "However, if you would think in English, that would be more helpful."

"No problem," Sassy said, hopping up and making the witchy duo a trio.

Zelda began.

· · ·

"GODDESS ON HIGH, HEAR MY CALL
My ball licking idiots have gone AWOL
Please send them a message to bring their fat asses home
Or I'll remove their peckers and umm... turn them to
Styrofoam."

"OHHHH, GOOD ONE," SASSY SAID. "MAKE SURE YOU SAY FUCK. It's the magic word."

"On it," Zelda replied.

"Seriously?" Zach asked, looking at both of them like they were insane.

"Dude, seriously," Zelda shot back with a grin. "Try it sometime. Occasionally the Goddess zaps my ass for my profanity, but secretly I think she loves it. Keeps her on her toes."

"Can I add to the spell?" Sassy asked.

"Go for it," Zelda said. "The more the merrier."

"HEY GODDESS ON HIGH
I have my wax by my side
If you don't find the furry fuckers
I'll dehair your big-ass, mom-jeans covered hide."

"SHIT," ZELDA SHOUTED AS LIGHTNING BLASTED THROUGH the ceiling from the Heavens above. "Take cover!"

Everyone dropped and scattered. However, the Goddess had excellent aim. Sassy's ass was now on fire.

"You think threatening to wax her crack was too much?" Sassy squealed, frantically scooting her smoldering bottom across the floor to put the flames out.

"I'm gonna go with a yes on that one," Zelda said, wiggling her fingers and dousing the flames. "You might want to ease up on the direct insults, dude."

"My ass says thanks for the advice," Sassy replied with a groan.

"Zach, would you like to finish up?" Zelda requested.

"Umm... no," he said, looking up at the charred hole in the ceiling and grinning in disbelief. "However, I will. Leaving it like that probably isn't wise."

"I second the motion," Mac said, from behind the chair.

"I'll go on record as a third," I volunteered from under the couch.

"Roger that," Zach said with a chuckle as he began.

GODDESS ON HIGH, SORRY ABOUT THAT,

Sassy's prowess with foreign language clearly fell a bit flat.
Please bring the cats home, our friends are in danger,
In your debt we shall be, and we'll work on Sassy's spells and make them less, umm... stranger.
So mote it be.

"STRONG FINISH," SASSY CONGRATULATED ZACH AS SHE rubbed her backside gingerly.

"How's your ass?" Zelda asked Sassy.

"Been better, but thankfully I'm going commando so I

didn't lose a good pair of panties," she replied and went back to work on the dollhouse.

Sassy's admission caused one minute and thirty-seven seconds of appalled silence. She was outstanding at stopping a conversation dead in its tracks.

"Will the spell work?" I asked, crawling out from under the couch.

"Eventually," Zelda said with a nod. "However, I have an idea of who might be able to help you in the meantime. Someone who has money to spare. He probably knows other people who have that kind of money and are stupid enough to throw it away on a shitty community theatre show."

Relief washed over me. "You do?"

"Who is it? Is he a criminal?" Zach questioned, eyeing his sister.

"Umm... define *criminal*," she said.

"Someone who breaks the law," Zach said dryly.

"Then yes," Zelda conceded with a goofy grin. "However, he's been toeing the line for a while now. I'd have to call him a reformed criminal who likes to steal from the rich and give to the poor."

"Like Robin Hood?" I asked, getting confused.

"Yep," Zelda said. "But with stickier fingers and very good taste in designer clothes."

"Name," Zach said. "Give me his name. Please."

Zelda gave her brother an odd look. "You're not gonna like the answer."

"Don't care," Zach said flatly. "Is it possible this person is the investor?"

"No way," Zelda said with absolute conviction. "The person I'm talking about loves Roger and Bob. He wouldn't harm a hair on what's left of Bob's unibrow."

"But he can help us?" Zach pressed.

"I believe so."

"Excellent," Zach said, blowing out a relieved sigh. "Give me his name. I'll deal with him myself."

"You will?" Zelda inquired casually. Way too casually. "You will *personally* deal with the idiot who has that kind of money and who could possibly save you from being a grunting kidney and protect Bob and Roger at the same time?"

Zach narrowed his eyes at his sister. They were the flip side of each other. Identical except for gender and height. She was up to something. That much was clear. But what she was up to was anyone's guess. Zelda was a nutbag.

"Yes," Zach hissed. "I will personally deal with someone who will help us make sure that no one puts cement shoes on Roger and Bob and throws them in the river. And if it means I don't have to grunt like a kidney, it will be well worth it."

"You're sure?" Zelda asked, smiling wider.

"Quite," Zach shot back. "Who is it?"

"He's the former artistic director of the Assjacket Theatre," she said cryptically. "He gave up the job recently because his batshit crazy gal pal likes to travel a lot."

"Awesome! Maybe he'll be more understanding," I said, unsure where the hell the conversation was going. "He can possibly help us convince the investor to let us make a payment plan. Or maybe he'll pay it and we can pay him back. I have 20K in the bank I can donate and I can start teaching botany again to make up the rest. Might take me a while, but I'm all in."

Zach glanced over at me and smiled. "You're beautiful."

A blush started at my chest and rose quickly to my cheeks.

"I have about fifty thousand in the bank," Zach said still smiling at me. "We can knock out the debt together."

"Together," I agreed.

"Yessssssssss," Zelda sang, looking between the two of us with delight.

"Not so fast, sister of mine," Zach said with a grin that matched hers. "Willow and I are taking baby steps and getting to know each other without a curse or a nightmare of a voodoo witch involved. Apparently, I need to like myself to win the hand of the dryad."

"Love," I corrected him with a raised brow.

"Impossible," he shot back with a grin.

"Nope. A tiny bit improbable. Not impossible," I reminded him. "And while you learn to love yourself, I'll find my hairy magical beans."

"Are you speaking Chinese?" Sassy asked, glancing up at me from the dollhouse.

"Yep, it means balls."

"As in the kind you bounce?" Sassy asked. "Or are we talking dangly bits, gangoolies, nickel ticklers, giggle berries, hanging fun bags…"

"Sweet Goddess in a boob tube and Bermuda shorts," Zelda shouted with her sparking hands aimed at Sassy. "I am going to zap you bald and give you a freaking tail, dude. Enough with the ball talk."

"One more?" Sassy requested with a wide grin.

Zelda rolled her eyes dramatically and smiled in spite of herself. "One. Only one."

Sassy giggled, stood up and took a small bow in advance of her final testicle term. "Wrinkled skin grapes," Sassy announced and then went right back to rearranging Audrey's dollhouse.

Mac laughed. "On that educational note, I'm going to check on the kids."

"I'll be up in a minute or two," Zelda told him with a wink.

I was pretty sure we'd interrupted naptime-nookie time. Damn, Zelda couldn't catch a break with all of us living here. We should probably see if there were any places to rent in Assjacket. Wearing out our welcome would be rude.

"Where's Zorro?" Sassy asked, looking around.

"He went back to the community center," Zach said, glancing at his watch. "Should've been here by now, but he probably got to talking to someone."

I nodded and put my arm around Zach's waist. I'd figured the same thing. Zorro could have a conversation with a wall and the wall would be ecstatic and forever in his fan club. Zorro was that charming.

Zelda turned her attention back to Zach and me, and squealed. She danced around the room and laughed like a crazy witch. "Baby steps with the dryad of your dreams," she said, pointing to Zach. "I love it. However, learning to love yourself is going to suck ass. Been there. Done that. I'd suggest going to Roger. You'll want to headbutt him, but he's really good—and I'll deny saying that."

"Done," Zach said, glancing down at me with a grin. "Willow has set us up for couples therapy."

"Jeeves and I did a few sessions with Roger," Sassy volunteered. "That little mother humpin' bunny made me realize that I'm not stupid, just a little left of centrality."

"You mean center?" I asked and then slapped my hand over my mouth, prepared to be horrified.

Just when I thought I had Sassy pegged....

"Nope," Sassy said. "Centrality. It's Swahili and means the quality of being essential or of great importance. So, it's okay that I'm not the sharpest broom in the linen closet. I'm still worthwhile."

Zelda walked over to Sassy and wrapped her arms around her. Whispering something in her ear, Sassy kissed Zelda's cheek and hugged her back. It was simple, real and beautiful. Their adoration of each other reminded me of Zorro's and my friendship.

"Enough of the sappy shit," Zelda said, disengaging herself from her BFF and zoning right back in on Zach and me. "In order to love yourself, you have to let go of shit."

"First of all, I'm going for *liking* myself before I can commit to getting into a deeper relationship with myself," Zach said with an eye roll that was as impressive as his sister's. "And what the hell does that have to do with anything?"

"A lot," she replied.

"Want to be less cryptic?" he inquired, getting annoyed.

"Dude, I've missed out on years of pissing you off," Zelda

complained. "Cut me some slack here. I'm having a good time."

"You are a complete pain in my ass," Zach said, trying to keep a straight face.

He failed.

"Thank you," Zelda replied as she did a horrifying rendition of the Running Man move. "I'm winning."

Zach laughed at his sister's excitement and ran his hands through his hair. "No more games. Who is the person who can help us?"

"Fabio."

Uh oh. This was not good… or maybe it was good.

"Your father?" Zach said, sounding incredibly tired.

"Our father," Zelda corrected him as she crossed her arms over her chest and watched her brother closely.

Zach paled slightly then glared at his sister. "I don't have a father, Zelda. I have a sperm donor to whom I owe nothing and he owes nothing in return," he said flatly. "I don't hate the man. I just don't want him in my life."

"Why? Zach, he didn't know about us," Zelda said softly.

Zach shrugged and a flash of pain crossed his expression so quickly, I wasn't sure that it had happened. However, his body went rigid. I could read his feelings of worthlessness loud and clear. "No reason," he said in a clipped tone. "Just is the way it is."

"Zach, you're right," I said as Zelda's eyes grew wide with disappointment and surprise. I held up my hand before she could contradict me. I continued, choosing my words carefully. "You owe Fabio nothing, nor does he owe you. But I think you owe it to *yourself* to at least get to know him a little bit. If you like him, great. If you don't, you lose nothing. However, there might be something to gain for both of you."

Zach ran his hands through his hair and expelled a very long slow breath. The tension in his body was obvious and his magic was very close to the surface. My warlock was a ticking time bomb of pain.

"The only thing to gain from the man is the name of the investor if he knows who it is, or at the very least a list of possibilities," Zach ground out between clenched teeth. "Other than that, I'd like to kick his ass."

"Mmkay, it's a start. Violence is an excellent jumping-off point," Zelda said. "Look, when he was my cat, I ran over him three times with my car and considered dropping him off at the pound before we worked it all out. Plus, I saw him naked. It was fucking horrifying. Took me forever to call him dad after seeing his junk. If you want, you can use the term Fabdudio—kind of a combo of Fabio and Dad. It works for me."

"I'll stick with Zelda's dad for the time being," Zach said.

"That works too," Zelda said with a grin. "He answers to pretty much anything."

"How about calling him Fabio?" I suggested, going for something that wouldn't incite a smackdown in the first two minutes of a meeting. "Or sperm donor, if Fabio is too personal. Our goal is to get a name so Bob and Roger don't die. Keep the end game in mind."

Zach turned to me. He looked like a lost child, unsure what to do. He didn't think he was good enough for Fabio in the same way he didn't think he was good enough for me.

My heart clenched and I immediately moved to him and held him tight. His body was stiff and unyielding. I hugged tighter and he finally relaxed and hugged me back.

"You make it all okay," he whispered. "You make me okay."

"No," I whispered back. "You will make you okay, and I will be here to love you while you figure it out."

"You'll come with me to see Zelda's dad?" he asked.

Smiling, I realized I'd lost the name war. It didn't matter. We were about to take the first baby step in Zach learning to love himself and letting shit go. If he ended up having a relationship with Fabio, that was wonderful. If he didn't, that was fine too as long as it was his choice and not because he didn't think he was worthy. "Yes, I will be at your side when you talk to Zelda's dad."

"Awesome," Zelda said, yanking Sassy up off of the floor and pushing all of us out the front door. "I need to get laid and you all need to get some names so we can start begging for Bob and Roger's lives. Here's Fabio's address. Have fun and let me know how it goes."

On that loving parting note, she shoved a piece of paper into Zach's hands and slammed the door shut on us.

"How about I go find Zorro and take him for a ride on my broom?" Sassy suggested.

"Umm... how about you find him and let him know we're going to see Fabio?" I countered. I'd seen Sassy fly. You couldn't pay me to get on her broom, and I certainly didn't wish that on my bestie.

"On it," Sassy said, hopping on her broom. "I'll find him and fly him over to my place for the evening so Zelda and

Mac can bang in peace. You guys go kick Fabio's butt and get some names. If we have names, I'll know who to wax. Remember to take pictures!" She zipped off and Zach and I watched her almost crash into a tree.

"She's going to wax the investor?" Zach asked, wincing as Sassy strafed the top of Sponge Bob then flew off towards town.

"Apparently," I said with a pained laugh. "Sassy's unique."

"And violent," Zach added.

I laughed again. "Says the man who wants to kick his sperm donor's ass."

Zach chuckled and shrugged. "I just..."

"You don't need to explain unless you want to," I told him.

He nodded and smiled. "You're perfect, Willow."

"Not even close," I said with a giggle.

"For me," Zach said softly. "You are perfect for me."

Zach leaned into me with clear intention in his eyes. My breath caught in my throat and I met him in the middle. I would always meet him in the middle. This was a little more than a baby step, but I couldn't resist the way the touch of his lips on mine made me feel. I melted into the kiss that I'd been waiting for my whole life.

As Zach deepened the kiss, the world fell away and my body tingled from head to toe. It was slow and insistent and passionate. The sounds he made sent my brain right to places that included far more than kissing. Our tongues tangled in a sensual dance and our bodies pressed so close there was no space left between us.

"Goddess, Willow," Zach said in a rough voice as he

pulled back from the kiss with effort. "I want you so badly it hurts."

I nodded jerkily. Speech was impossible. My heart pounded so loudly in my chest, I was sure all of Assjacket could hear it. I was on Cloud Nine and wasn't coming down any time soon.

"Now, it's up to me to deal with my shit and get into a semi-functional relationship with myself," he said, gently cupping my cheek in his hand. "I can't promise to have a relationship with Fabio like Zelda has, but my sister is correct. I need to let shit go. We're starting now. You with me?" he asked, looking worried.

"All the way," I told him, turning my head and kissing the palm of his hand. "I'm in all the way."

CHAPTER TEN

Zelda's dad's house was lovely. It had previously belonged to his dearly departed and much-loved sister Hildy—a healer witch like Zelda, Zach and Fabio. Hildy had left the house to Zelda in her will, and Zelda had given it to her dad when she'd mated with Mac and moved into his place.

My breath caught in my throat when I saw it. It was as if the house had walked straight out of my dreams and plopped itself down in Assjacket, West Virginia. The white Victorian had a wraparound porch dotted with rocking chairs and charming turrets. Perfumed wildflowers and rose bushes covered the grounds and huge trees shaded the beautiful home. Touching one of the large oaks, I smiled. The trees were happy here. I could feel their contented hum.

"He doesn't know we're coming," Zach said tightly,

taking in the house and the property. His tension was through the roof. "This is a very bad plan."

"Did Zelda give you his phone number?" I asked, pulling out my phone. "We could hide in the trees and call him. See if he's home."

At that very moment, Fabio walked out of the front door and stood on the porch. His handsome face was so like his son's. The smile he wore was tentative and unsure, but it was welcoming.

"Don't think we have to call," I said with a quick, friendly wave to Fabio. I took Zach's hand and pulled him toward the house.

It was similar to dragging a cement boulder.

"He doesn't bite," I whispered.

"Right," Zach said. "And if he does, I'll zap the shit out of him."

"Good plan," I said with a laugh.

Zach's steps slowed. "I feel strange." He sounded more like a little boy than a grown man.

I stopped tugging him along and stared up into his sparkling green eyes. They were the same eyes as the man on the porch who watched our every move. "I can talk to Fabio if you want to stay here."

Zach shook his head and blew out a resigned breath. "No. We're here for Bob and Roger. I'm not here for a come to the Goddess with my sperm donor. I can do this."

"For Bob and Roger," I repeated and waited for him to move. I was here for Zach and would approach the house when he was ready.

"I'm good," Zach said, nodding to Fabio and striding forward. "Gonna let go of some shit."

I just hoped letting go of shit didn't involve blood or broken bones—or Goddess forbid, getting mowed down by a car. But while warlocks were strong, dryads packed a pretty powerful magical punch. However, we were here to get a name, not play happy families. Even so, I loved Zach and had very strong feelings of like for Fabio, so I was also going to make sure, whatever happened, everyone saw tomorrow in one piece.

THE INTERIOR OF THE HOUSE WAS AS LOVELY AS THE EXTERIOR —hardwood floors with colorful Persian rugs. The furniture was overstuffed and comfortable. The windows stretched from the floor to the ceiling and the natural light was fabulous. The only oddity was an enormous disco ball that hung from the ceiling in the foyer. It was garish and hilarious, but somehow fit in perfectly.

"How much?" Fabio questioned.

"They paid Mae Blockinschlokinberg two hundred thousand dollars," I told him then gasped in disbelief as Fabio snapped his fingers and a mountain of money appeared.

Loads of cash—all hundred-dollar bills—sat atop of the distressed oak kitchen table that seated twelve. There was far more than two hundred thousand.

The sunlight streaming through the windows illuminated and framed the stack of bills as I gaped at them in shock. I'd never seen so much money in my life. As soon as we'd told Fabio the horrible story from beginning to end, he was on it. No questions were asked other than how much money we needed.

Zach cleared his throat and stared at the bills. I was fairly sure he had never seen that much cash either.

"Actually, Zelda's dad," Zach said. "We're only looking for a name."

Fabio pushed the pile over to Zach's and my side of the table and shook his head. "I have no clue who could have been stupid enough to invest that much money in the Assjacket Community Theatre," he said with a laugh.

"Umm… you're about to invest that much right now," I said, pointing at the cash. "I mean, we'll pay you back, but it might take a decade or ten."

"*Absolu-tree* not," Fabio said with a smile, charming me with his Puntreelish. "I don't need it or want it back."

Zach stared at the man who was the mirror image of himself. "Can I ask where you got this kind of money, Zelda's dad?"

Fabio grew wildly fascinated with his cuticles. I almost laughed. This entire family was an intriguing hot mess.

"Is that a literal question or a figurative one?" he queried.

Zach looked down at the table to hide what I thought might be a smile. "Literal."

Fabio ran his hands through his hair until it stood on end. It was clear he was contemplating how much to share. The moment was as achingly important to him as it was to Zach. I knew it even if Zach didn't want to acknowledge it. Fabio had been hiding in the woods trying to get close to Zach for a month, for the love of the Goddess.

It might have been easier if he'd actually come out of the woods and spoken to his son, but warlocks were an odd bunch.

"Mmkay," Fabio said, sitting up straighter in his chair in an attempt to look professional and sincere. "Is lying acceptable or would that be a problem for you?"

"Are you serious?" Zach asked, squinting at Fabio.

"Of course not," Fabio insisted, laughing way too hard. "I was joking... kind of."

"Did you procure it... umm... legally?" I asked with a wince, trying to help Fabio out.

"*Interesting* you should ask... Could you define legal?" Fabio inquired politely, looking like he was constipated.

"Again," Zach said, tilting his head and examining Fabio like he was a science experiment gone wrong. "Are you serious?"

Fabio expelled a long breath, propped his elbows on the table and rested his forehead in his hands. "Unfortunately, yes," he muttered sadly with his face hidden. "I'm not the father you may have dreamed of, Zach. I'm not exactly responsible parental material. However, I want it to be very clear I had no clue I'd knocked up your rancid excuse of a mother. I was a little wild back in the day. But back to the matter at hand, I must admit, I've had numerous run-ins with the law over minor, inconsequential, ridiculous and teeny-weeny infractions."

"Such as?" Zach was now smiling, but since Fabio's face was still hidden, he had no clue.

"Well, there was a minuscule bit of gambling and the occasional identity theft of those who abused power. It was delightful to bankrupt asshole dictators and spread their wealth amongst the people they'd screwed over. Kind of like an orgasm without the sex," Fabio admitted. "Oh, and grand larceny, but for a good cause."

"Good cause?" I asked, liking the man even more. His methods were certainly questionable, but his heart was in the right place.

"School busses," he whispered. "For a community that had none."

"How many?" Zach inquired, staring at the top of his father's head.

"Twenty-five," Fabio whispered. "And I might have manipulated the lotto a few times."

"So that you won?" I asked, surprised.

"Oh dear Goddess, no!" Fabio said, looking up at me aghast. "Using magic for personal gain is a huge no-no. For others who needed it. And of course, I have a wee collection of what one might refer to as hot credit cards. I've also been known to procure the latest fashions before they actually hit the market, but I leave an IOU or brownies."

"You leave *brownies*?" Zach asked, obviously unsure if Fabio was sane.

He wasn't, but that was part of the charm.

"Not the little girls in the brown uniforms," Fabio assured us quickly. "The chocolate kind… with nuts."

Zach coughed to hide his laugh. "Anything else I should know?"

Fabio sighed dramatically. "Yes, I suppose there is. I'm an

excellent cook, and I find women's yoga pants very comfortable. I'm in a committed relationship for the first time in my life with Baba Yaga. She's completely off her rocker and prone to blowing up things, but I am besotted—hence the appalling disco ball in the foyer. Also, I find a good explosion to be excellent foreplay."

"Keep going," Zach said, unable to hide his perplexed amusement.

Fabio gained confidence from Zach's tone and barreled on. "Your sister loves my pancakes even though she offends them with an obscene amount of syrup. I spent a decade in the circus in between running from the law and being a man-whore. Juggling was my specialty—balls and women. Baba Yaga, aka Carol, put an end to that. She's threatened to remove my balls if I stray but, quite honestly, I never will. Mostly, before I found happiness, I tooled around aimlessly and gambled. I'm an outstanding card cheater... And then, one day, it all got very old and I searched for meaning." He took a breath. "At over two hundred years old, I realized I had very little worth to show for my existence on the Goddess's green earth. When I found out about your sister, I was thrilled and then devastated to learn what she had gone through in her life. It took a bit to get close, including a few near-deadly car mishaps and then an embarrassing reveal of my man-junk, but I paid for her therapy. So, there's that."

Zach said nothing, but his body relaxed. He watched Fabio and waited for more.

"I blamed myself for Zelda's horrific start in life... and I blame myself for yours," Fabio said quietly.

"But you didn't know about us," Zach said and then pressed the bridge of his nose in annoyance.

Defending the man who he didn't want in his life wasn't in the game plan, but Zach was a good person, whether he believed it or not. He was very much like the warlock sitting across from him, minus the criminal record.

"I didn't know," Fabio agreed. "But it doesn't alleviate the guilt. It never will. I'm so sorry."

I said nothing. It wasn't my place, but my heart hurt, and I wanted to hug both men so badly my fingers tingled. So much pain because of one horrible woman who'd raised Zelda in an awful manner and who had sold Zach as a baby to an abomination.

Fabio went on. "I understand if you can't accept me, and I don't blame you. I'm not exactly a prize. But I just want you to know that if I could have traded places with you, I would have in a heartbeat. And if Henrietta Smith wasn't already dead, I would have taken obscene pleasure in ending her with my bare hands."

Zach's mouth was slightly open as if he wanted to speak, but no words came out. Fabio gave him a sad smile and pointed to the money.

"Most of it is legal," he said. "Please take it. I don't want it back. It's just a tiny gesture. I would be pleased if you would use it. It can't make up for the past, but I can ease your future and keep Bob and Roger safe. Plus, I'd be horrified if you had to be a grunting kidney."

Zach laughed.

It was a gorgeous sound.

And the look on Fabio's face was one I wouldn't forget. He literally glowed with pride at having made his son smile.

"Look… umm… Fabio," Zach said, stepping way out of his comfort zone. "I'm sorry too and while you might have a criminal record, I have much worse. If you knew what I'd done in my life, you wouldn't be so excited to have a relationship with me."

I couldn't stop myself. I didn't want to, so I didn't. "It wasn't you. It was her—Henrietta Smith," I insisted, wanting to cry in anger and frustration. "You were cursed, sold and used. Your choices were taken from you."

Zach put his hand over mine and squeezed it gently. Closing his eyes, he let out a choppy breath. "People died and I did nothing. I watched. She killed and I abetted."

"Bullshit," Fabio said. "I call bullshit."

Zach eyed him angrily. "I don't care what you call. Shifters, witches and warlocks died and I did nothing," he ground out through clenched teeth.

"Were you capable of defending them?" Fabio demanded, standing his ground.

"Does it matter?" Zach snapped. "Hundreds are dead."

"*It matters,*" Fabio shot right back, equally as harsh. "What was done to you would have destroyed a lesser man. It tears at my soul to know what you lived through, but you are *not* to blame. Henrietta Smith was a deranged and sorry excuse of a fake witch who followed a sham religion not recognized by the Goddess. What she did is on her, not you. Never you," Fabio said firmly. "You are as much a victim as those she destroyed."

"Fairytales are lies and very hard to swallow," Zach said,

sounding so much older than his years. "Yes, it's true I was helpless to stop her. But a lifetime of watching needless death takes a toll."

"Let that shit go," Fabio said, staring at Zach with an intensity that was captivating. "If you need to pay a self-imposed penance, pay it. For every evil atrocity that woman did, do something kind, loving and semi-legal to replace it. And no... it will not bring her victims back, but it will slowly make the Goddess's Universe a more beautiful place. Do good in the memory of those who can't. You've already started."

Zach rubbed his temples and eyed his father. "You're quite smart for a criminal."

"Thank you. I try," Fabio replied with a charming grin. "It's a wondrous and strange thing... I love you, Zach. I can't explain it correctly, but I look at you and I see a beautiful, virtuous man."

Zach tensed at Fabio's admission, but he didn't punch him. I took it as a good sign.

"Then you need glasses, old man. I'm not worthy of your love," Zach said flatly.

"My choice to give," Fabio said. "Your choice to accept."

"Can't yet," Zach admitted. "Working on a relationship with myself. Willow is next in line. You're in fourth place behind Zelda."

Fabio grinned and clapped his hands. "I'll take it and you will take the money. Please take the money."

I shook my head in agreement with Zach. "Honestly, Fabio, the money doesn't help until we know who the investor is," I told him. "Besides, even if we pay him off, there's no guarantee he won't want retribution for the community theatre not producing the play. But thank you. It's such an incredible and kind offer."

"Willow is right," Zach said. "Do you have any idea who might have put that kind of money up?"

Fabio's brow wrinkled in thought. "I truly don't," he said. "However, once we discover who he is, the money is ready if he'll take it."

"*We?*" Zach inquired with a raised brow.

Fabio grinned. "If you're dealing with someone who's fond of cement shoes, I would think having a criminal like myself on your team might be helpful."

Again, Zach laughed.

Again, Fabio beamed.

My smile grew so wide it hurt my cheeks.

Zach sobered and focused on Fabio. "I'm not sure what kind of relationship we can have," he said slowly, clearly finding his words as the thoughts came. "But I would like to start as friends."

Fabio's breath caught in his throat and his sparkling green eyes teared up. "I would like that very much. Also, if you'd like to run me over with a car, I'm in. It did wonders for your sister."

"Thank you, but I'll pass," Zach said with a chuckle. "I thought I wanted to punch you before I came, but…"

"Let's go," Fabio bellowed joyously, jumping up from his chair. "We can duke it out in the front yard. It will be good for the soul."

"Umm… I don't know," I said, wondering how they went from being friends to kicking each other's asses.

"Seriously?" Zach asked, excited. "You'll punch back, right?"

"Of course," Fabio said. "I'd be honored to have a smackdown with my son. We've missed out on so much."

"So much violence?" I asked, still not thinking this was a great plan.

"Yes!" Fabio said. "A father should teach his son how to fight. A little blood and a few broken bones are a byproduct of the love warlocks share. Very stupid and manly, but quite fun."

"Sounds great," Zach said, grinning.

"Outstanding! We can heal each other afterward," Fabio said, ushering us through the kitchen and out the front door. "And if the injuries are too much for male warlock healers to handle, we'll call your sister. Zelda will definitely take blackmail photos, but she's the strongest healer witch in existence. If she balks, I'll withhold the new Berkin bag I procured for her."

"Good plan," Zach said, following Fabio out of the front door as I stood rooted to the floor in shock.

"Come along, Willow," Fabio called over his shoulder. "A good time shall be had by all."

"Coming," I muttered, forcing my feet to move. Warlocks were batshit crazy.

"Oh, and I'd be quite honored if you two would stay for dinner and spend the night," Fabio offered, looking wildly unsure of Zach's reaction. "I'll cook and there are many spare bedrooms to choose from."

"Willow?" Zach asked, as unsure as his father. "Does that sound good?"

Staring at Zach, I knew he wanted to accept, but wanted me to go first. Not happening. I winked at him and let him swim in the deep end on his own. "Your choice."

He eyed me askance for a second and then smiled. He had my number and I had his.

"Yes, Fabio," he said. "We will take you up on the offer."

"I'll let Zelda know!" Fabio shouted with such an over-abundance of joy it made me giggle.

It was perfect. Sassy was bringing Zorro to her place, and we would stay with Fabio. Mac and Zelda would have an evening with no company present. They could have a nookie night all over the house.

"Shall we?" Zach asked his father, his eyes glittering with excitement and his fists raised.

"Yes," Fabio replied, getting into an attack position and grinning back at his son. "We shall."

The fight would be seared into my brain for eternity. As the two warlocks beat the living crap out of each other, they laughed like children having the time of their lives. Even the trees enjoyed the show. They swayed and rustled their leaves with glee. Of course, it was clear that the brawl was all in good violent fun...

The joy and excitement the men shared as they traded blows was strangely beautiful—albeit in a bloody and profanity-filled way. But their bond strengthened with each powerful punch. In the end, the two battered warriors held each other, laughed like idiots, and healed each other's broken bones and bruises.

All in all, it was a successful visit. We didn't have the name of the investor, but we knew we had the money to pay him back if push came to shove. I felt calmer than I had earlier. Hopefully, the cats were on their way home and Mae Blockinschlokinberg would accept her firing without a countersuit or counterattack.

And of course, until that was a go, we'd go on with rehearsals.

Let the shitshow continue.

CHAPTER ELEVEN

THE DAY DAWNED BRIGHT AND SUNNY AND MY MOOD matched. Fabio's home was as magical as Zelda's. I was pretty sure I never wanted to *leaf* Assjacket. With so much love and so many wonderful people, it was perfect. Even the crazy was wonderful and glorious.

"Oh my Goddess," I said with a mouthful as I stacked two more pancakes on my plate. "These are delicious."

"Thank you," Fabio said, taking a small bow. "I can make more. And I must say, it's a real pleasure to watch you two enjoy my pancakes without a vat of syrup on them. Zelda's palate is just horrid."

Patting my full stomach, I laughed. "I'm good with these. I'm about to pop."

"I'll take a few more," Zach said much to Fabio's delight.

We'd stayed up talking till the early morning hours. It had been a wonderful night mixed with laughter and tears. Zach had spoken more candidly about his past. I learned things that made me feel ill. I didn't think my hatred of Henrietta Smith could eclipse what it already was, but I was wrong. Fabio looked as if he'd been shredded from the inside out as he'd listened to his son recount his tortured past, but it was healing for Zach. Both Fabio and I would have listened to the very same stories over and over for the man we loved.

However, not all of it was serious. Zach and I learned how to cheat at cards, and Fabio made me laugh till I almost cried while telling stories about his great love, Baba Yaga.

Of course, I knew who she was, but had never met her. Baba Yaga, the leader of the witches and warlocks, instilled a healthy fear in everyone, but Fabio's adoration of the most powerful witch in the Universe made her seem so normal— in an abnormal way. I couldn't wait to meet her.

"So, Willow," Fabio said, sitting down at the table after heaping Zach's plate with enough pancakes for a small army. "Have you located your nards yet?"

I was glad I didn't have food in my mouth since I choked on my reply. "Umm... no, but I'll find them," I assured him.

"I don't think you ever lost them," Zach said, looking at me with so much love in his expression, I blushed. "You have enormous magical hairy beans."

We'd run into a conundrum last night at bedtime. As much as we'd wanted to share a room, the time wasn't right yet—there was still more work to do and we had our sessions with Roger soon. Instead, we'd made out in the hallway like teenagers until we were busted by a delighted Fabio. Going to sleep knowing Zach was across the hall was incredibly difficult, but in the end, I'd slept… and dreamed of my handsome warlock.

When the time did arrive, it was going to rock our world.

"You know," Fabio pointed out thoughtfully. "Not sure why anyone would want testicles when a vagina is so much stronger."

"Umm… Fabio," Zach said with a wince. "Not really breakfast table talk."

Fabio raised his hand and grinned. "Hear me out. The slightest flick to the nards can send even the strongest man to his knees. Whereas a vagina can push out an entire small human. In my book, balls are much weaker than the bits you were born with, Willow."

My mouth hung open and my eyes grew wide. Yes, it was seriously embarrassing to have a conversation about vaginas and testicles with the father of the man I was in love with, but he'd made a shockingly good point.

Did I even need balls?

"Wow," I muttered when I could find my voice. "That was profound—a little graphic, but profound."

Fabio laughed. "I'm good like that—very dangerous at parties, though."

"Maybe your umm… parts are your lady balls," Zach said, as his cheeks reddened a bit. "I'd have to agree with Fabio that nuts are overrated."

"And quite unattractive," Fabio added, clearing our plates. "Lady bits are lovely."

"You can stop any time now," Zach said with an eye roll.

"Whoops," Fabio said. "This is why no one wants me at parties."

"Rightly so," Zach said, chuckling. "You have no filter."

"Comes with age," Fabio agreed. "So, we have rehearsal this morning?"

"You're coming?" I asked.

"Indeed, I am," he replied with a wicked little grin. "As the former artistic director of the Assjacket Community Theatre, I have every right to be there. And this Mae Block-inschlokinberg seems like she needs a few hard truths explained to her."

"I like it," Zach said, standing up and stretching his muscular body in a way that made me ache to jump on it. "Are you comfortable with me calling you Fabio in public?"

Fabio beamed. "I'll answer to anything you'd like to call me," he promised. "You wouldn't believe the names I've been called over the years."

"Actually, I probably would," Zach said.

Fabio grinned from ear to ear. "Fine point. Well made. Shall we go?"

Snapping my fingers, I replaced my dress from yesterday with a sharp, lime green Stella McCartney mini dress.

"Hang on!" Fabio squealed as he sprinted out of the room.

"What just happened?" I asked Zach.

"No clue," Zach replied with a grin. "He's insane."

"And pretty great," I added.

Zach paused for a moment and stared at his hands. "Yes. He's pretty great."

Fabio flew back into the room with a gorgeous chocolate

brown leather Birkin bag that made my mouth water. "For you! It will be fabulous with that dress."

I wanted it so badly, my fingers itched, but... "I thought that was for Zelda."

"Darling Willow, I procured six. I always have a few extras lying around. Never know when I need to gift a beautiful bag to a beautiful gal."

"Define procure," Zach said dryly.

"Literally or figuratively?" Fabio questioned.

"Forget it," Zach said, taking my hand in his. "Did you leave brownies?"

"I most certainly did," Fabio said grandly. "Six dozen. One dozen for each bag and I added extra nuts."

"You're extra nuts." Zach shook his head and sighed in amusement.

The rich, soft leather of the bag was heavenly in my hands. Giving Fabio a quick kiss on the cheek, I grinned at Zach. "I'm sure his brownies are as delicious as his pancakes. I think it's a fair trade."

Zach pulled me close and kissed me. "Are we ready to face the day?"

"We are," I said, my lips already missing his. "Shall we poof over?"

"Yep, let's poof," Fabio said. "It's faster."

And poof we did.

We poofed right into a shitshow of epic proportions.

And not the one we'd expected.

CHAPTER TWELVE

We arrived to a surprise and not a good one.

"I heard it sucked!" a woman gleefully and maliciously called across the room to another.

"Can't wait! I just adore mass humiliation," her nasty buddy shouted back.

Shit. Something was very wrong—*tree-mendously* wrong. My stomach clenched, and I glanced around in distress for my friends. Not one was in sight.

The large hall was packed with people, wall to wall—at least two hundred. Some milled around and gossiped viciously while others had seated themselves in anticipation of I didn't even know what. It was *ex-tree-mely* unsettling. There was a rabid excitement and the aroma of flop sweat in the air that didn't bode well.

Fabio took in the crowd with a perplexed expression. "Is it possible that Mae Blockinschlokinberg added hundreds of cast members to *Jaws: The Musical*? Or, perhaps, she replaced all of you."

"Doubtful," Zach said as he steered us away from a trio of sour-faced witches and avoided getting us tripped by a group of jerky Shifters who were sticking their feet out then laughing hysterically when someone went down.

"What the heck is going on?" I asked, pushing through the rude crowd trying to reach the stage. It was a bummer to realize Assjacket had unpleasant citizens. Up until now, everyone had been awesome.

"Don't know," Zach said tightly, grabbing my hand and drawing me close so I didn't get swallowed up in the masses.

Fabio paled to the point I thought he might pass out. "No. Oh Goddess, no, no, no," he choked out, pointing to the group seated in the front row. The seats were filled with umm... men—or at least I thought it was men—wearing make-up, black turtlenecks, berets and unattractive smug smiles.

They held court for a bevy of screaming fans, signing autographs and posing for pictures.

"Who are those... women?" Zach asked, putting his arm around his father so he didn't drop to the ground like a sack of potatoes.

"Not women," Fabio said in a hushed and horrified tone. "It's the Tennessee Man-Titty Thespians."

"That's actually what they're called?" I asked. I was sure Sassy had made that one up.

"Look at them," Fabio hissed. "Of course, they're called the Man-Titty Thespians. I'd recognize those enormous man knockers and berets from a mile away. You'd think they'd have the decency to wear bras, but nooooo. Who could have done something so dastardly? This will ruin the Assjacket Community Theatre. Bob will be devastated. I'm not sure he'll recover from this kind of humiliation."

"Wait," Zach said, trying not to laugh while expertly navigating us toward the stage. "Men with boobs and berets can ruin Bob's life?"

"Zach," Fabio said, quickly pulling us to the backstage area and out of the mob of strangers. "Yes, those men with over-sized mammaries can wreck poor Bob's life. It seems small and quite honestly humorous, but you have to realize that Bob lives for his art. He's dreadful, but it fulfills him in a way nothing else other than his unibrow can. When I directed the musical version of *Mommie Dearest*, I came to a few realizations. One, *Mommie Dearest* was a terrible choice for a musical, and I never should have cast Bob as Christopher. The beaver had such stage fright he refused to step one foot out of the wings. Sassy covered for him, but that's a story for another time and will require copious amounts of alcohol to rehash. Number two, there's exquisite beauty in mediocre or no talent at all if the passion behind it is true. Bob's passion is from his heart. Will he ever be on Broadway? Goddess no, but he's free to stink up the stage in Assjacket and be adored like a movie star by everyone in town—everyone who loves him for who he is."

"Got it," Zach said, no longer smiling. "However, I still have no idea what's happening and why all these people are here."

Fabio peeked from behind the curtain and out at the full house. "I don't recognize any of them. It's bizarre."

"They're not Assjackians?" I asked, wildly relieved that the revolting assemblage wasn't from these parts.

"Not even one," Fabio said.

I looked around. "Where do you think Bob and the gang are?"

"Let's check the dressing rooms," Fabio said.

"There are dressing rooms?" Zach asked, confused.

Fabio nodded and beckoned us to follow. "Of course, there are. They double as food storage for the Shifter daycare the rest of the year, but we use them as changing rooms when we do shows. It works out nicely. Lots of applesauce and cookies if you get hungry."

"Wait," I said, pulling both men to a halt. "Mae Blockin-schlokinberg had to have done this to get back at Bob. She was furious about being fired so she invited the who's who of the community theatre world to demolish the reputation of the Assjacket Community Theatre. My guess is that she's going to force us to perform."

Fabio gasped and leaned against the wall. "Is there even a show to perform?"

Zach laughed. It held no trace of humor in it. "Hell to the no."

We stood in silence and plotted.

"We have to get rid of the audience," I said.

"You're right. Want me to pull a fire alarm?" Zach suggested.

"No," Fabio replied. "Once they realize it's a hoax, they'll come right back in. Those man-titties are out for blood."

"Well, crap," I said, trying to think of something else. "We could try poofing them away, but there are an awful lot of people out there for the three of us to poof."

Zach nodded. "Plus, we have no clue where they came from. Don't even know where to poof them back to."

"We could send the Tennessee Man-Titty Thespians to a clinic for breast reduction surgery," I said, then slapped my hand over my mouth. "Sorry, that was mean. They might be lovely people."

"They're not," Fabio assured me with a chuckle and a bit of a naughty gleam in his eye.

Crap. I hope he didn't make the knocker removal a reality. I'd feel terrible. Mean or no, if they loved their man bosoms, they should be able to keep them.

"Any other thoughts?" Zach asked.

"Yes." Fabio looked at me as a smile began to pull at his lips. "Go sing to them, Willow. Send them on their way. If you truly want nards, this will earn them for you."

My eyes widened and I laughed. Fabio was as dastardly as Mae Blockinschlokinberg, but in a much more hilarious and creative way.

Zach gave me a confused look. "I thought you couldn't sing. When Roger asked, you said you couldn't."

"Actually, I said I *shouldn't* sing," I reminded Zach. "I can sing, but the results are kind of…"

"X-rated," Fabio finished my sentence.

Zach's brow raised with interest, and he waited for an explanation.

"Dryads descended from Sirens," I explained hastily. "If I sing, I can make the entire crowd uncomfortably… umm…"

143

"Horny," Fabio supplied as my face heated in embarrassment. "And if they're horny and have even a shred of decency, they'll skedaddle on out to scratch their itch in private. It's a win-win. If I used magic, I'd be tempted to pop the Tennessee Man-Titty Thespians bosoms like ticks due to Willow's outstanding idea. But I suppose just because they're vulgar, braless, rude and wearing berets doesn't mean they should be disfigured. However, it would be greatly satisfying, especially since the bastards panned my last show."

Fabio had a little bit of Sassy's talent for colorful rants. Zach and I were speechless for a brief moment.

Finding my voice to reinforce Fabio's decision not to pop the man-knockers, I complimented him. I didn't want to be responsible in any way for deflated bosoms. "I think that's very big of you to let the thespians keep their boobs."

"Yes, I agree," Fabio said with complete sincerity. "You'll sing, then?"

"It's safe for you to do that?" Zach asked, worried, yet still intrigued by my newly discovered talent.

"Yep," I replied. "It's my choice if I want them to be aroused by me or by others."

Zach's ears had perked up along with his interest. "And what happens if you choose yourself?"

I wanted to melt into the floor. Zach's *father* was present. This was all kinds of weird.

"Umm… I don't know," I admitted. "Never tried it."

Fabio backed away and pretended to find something on the wall fascinating. Of course, he could still hear us, but it was the polite thought that counted.

Zach turned to me and pressed his forehead to mine, his hands resting on my hips. "I'd be willing to be your first test case," he said, sending tingles all through my body.

"I believe that could be arranged," I replied, wanting to jump his hot bod and kiss him senseless.

However, now was not a good time.

"Raincheck?" I asked with a lustful glint in my eyes that matched my warlock's.

"Definitely," he replied. "Soon."

"We done here, kids?" Fabio inquired with a huge grin.

"Umm… yes," I said with a giggle. Snapping my fingers, I conjured up noise-canceling earphones for Fabio and Zach. Making them horny was counterproductive to our plans. "Put these on," I instructed. "This won't take me but a minute."

"MY GODDESS," FABIO GASPED OUT, HIS EYES STILL FILLED with tears from laughing. "Never seen anything quite like that."

Zach shook his head and grinned. "I'm going to have to get some extra sessions with Roger to wipe that out of my brain."

Slapping my hands on my hips, I glared at the dummies and tried not to laugh. "They're gone. Right?"

"Definitely gone," Zach said, scrubbing his hands over his mouth to hide his shock and amusement.

It had literally taken only one verse of *Sexual Healing* by Marvin Gaye to get the crowd sprinting out of the building to find a hotel room. Thankfully, Assjacket didn't have a hotel and the stimulated horde had to leave town if they wanted to alleviate their symptoms with any amount of privacy.

Of course, the desperate dash out of the community center was a comedy of errors. The Tennessee Man-Titty Thespians blacked a few eyes of the other patrons with their braless bosoms in the race to find relief. Several of the vicious gossipers, who I was fairly sure were unacquainted, were swapping spit with each other as if their lives depended on it. Served them right for talking smack about the Assjacket Community Theatre. I choked with laughter as I watched a Thespian dive straight through a glass window since there was a backup of humping Shifters at the door. Honestly, singing was a handy weapon that I'd never used all that much.

As far as gaining nards from it... I'd have to say I didn't. However, I was no longer searching for my magical hairy beans. I had something even better. My va-jay-jay was far superior.

"Should we find our people?" Fabio suggested, wiping a stray tear of laughter from his eye.

"Yes," I said, quite proud of myself. "I'm worried."

"Hey," Zach said, pulling me back as Fabio marched toward the dressing rooms. "I want you to sing for me."

I raised my brow and crossed my arms over my chest. "I need to sing to get into your pants?"

"All you need to do is breathe in my direction, and I will happily give you my pants and anything else you want," Zach replied with a wink. "I just thought it would be fun."

146

"Deal," I replied, grabbing his hand and following after Fabio. "As soon as you love yourself, I'll sing to you."

"Getting there," Zach informed me with a lopsided grin. "I can truthfully say I like myself."

Life was good and definitely getting more interesting.

CHAPTER THIRTEEN

Bob was bald, unibrow-less, and as pale as a ghost.

Roger wasn't faring much better. His nose twitched a mile a minute, and his body trembled.

Sassy flew around the food storage/dressing room on her broom in complete agitation while Mae Blockinschlokinberg screamed like a banshee and her icky minions stood off to the side taking pictures.

Zorro was nowhere to be found.

"When I told you I couldn't be fired, I meant it," Mae Blockinschlokinberg snarled. "I will take you down along with this terrible little town."

"Not so fast," Zach growled as he strode into the room, interrupting the vicious dressing down in progress.

Fabio stood in the shadows by the doorway and watched with a furious expression on his face. The insane, disgustingly dressed woman didn't even notice him.

"It's about time," Mae Blockinschlokinberg snapped at

Zach and me. "You're late. You will be fined a thousand dollars for your first infraction. Second infraction will garner both of you a body boiling in a kettle full of snakes. Am I clear?"

"As mud," I snapped, wiggling my fingers and giving Bob a nice full unibrow and a headful of hair. "The audience left."

"WHAT?" Mae Blockinschlokinberg screamed so loudly I slapped my hands over my ears. "I paid a large sum to humiliate you people and create great art. You will reimburse me and add it to my salary." Reaching into the pocket of her muumuu and whipping out the check that Roger had paid her, she shoved it in his face. "Write one for three hundred thousand, rabbit. This one is no longer acceptable."

Sassy divebombed Mae Blockinschlokinberg and grabbed the check from her hand. Stuffing it into her mouth, she chewed and swallowed it. "You snooze, you lose, Mae Blockinschlokinbutthole. I ate your salary."

"Spit it out," the heinous woman screeched.

"Can't," Sassy told her with a laugh. "In an hour or so I could probably return it, but not sure you'd want it then."

Mae Blockinschlokinberg advanced on Roger, hissing and spitting with fury. He squeaked and shrank back in fear. Zach moved quickly to cut her off, but to everyone's surprise, Bob stepped up. His face was bright red with anger, and he huffed and puffed. With each exhale, his fluffy unibrow fluttered. In his distress, Bob began his shift, but not completely. His two front beaver teeth popped out and his tiny hands became furry with claws. In any other situation, I might have giggled. Right now, I was as proud as I imagined any mother figure would be.

"You go, Bob," I yelled, giving him a thumbs up. "You've got this."

Bob nodded and puffed out his little chest. His unibrow twitched and he gnashed his teeth. "You are out of luck, Mae Blockinschlokinshitbrick. We have no more checks, and it takes months to order a new batch with all of the paperwork and the lack of enthusiasm from the Assjacket Postmistress."

"Wait," Sassy said, hovering in the air on her broom. "I thought I was the Assjacket Postmistress. Am I? I can't remember."

"You are," Bob confirmed with a wince. "You're doing a wonderful job."

"Thank you!" Sassy said, beaming. "I didn't even remember that I had the job. Someone probably sent me the contract and it was in Canadian. Not to worry. I'll get right to work as soon as I figure out what I'm supposed to do. Cool?"

"Lovely," Bob replied.

Mae Blockinschlokinberg was boiling like she was going to blow. I considered zapping earplugs into my friends' ears and singing again. It would be a hilarious and humiliating payback to see Mae Blockinschlokinberg and her posse hump each other, but something else was wrong here. There was a distinct lack of fabulous in the room.

"Where's Zorro?" I asked, glancing around.

Mae Blockinschlokinberg smiled. It wasn't pretty. She

pulled a piece of paper from her pocket and waved it in the air. "He quit. Left a note and left town."

"Bullshit," Zach said, narrowing his eyes dangerously at the woman. "Zorro would not leave Assjacket without telling us."

"Well, he did," she informed him with sadistic satisfaction.

"Sassy," I said, feeling sick to my stomach. "Zorro was supposed to be with you."

"Wait. I thought he was with you," Sassy replied, getting slightly hysterical.

"Why would he be with us?" I asked, snatching the note out of Mae Blockinschlokinberg's hand. "You were supposed to find him and bring him to your house for the night so Zelda and Mac could bang in peace."

Sassy pulled on her hair and flew right into the wall, sending a pyramid of applesauce crashing to the ground. "Shit," she cried out as she slid to the floor and landed in the mess. The packets exploded, and we were all covered in mushy apple. "He wasn't at the community center when I went looking for him. I figured he went back to Zelda's. She said you guys were staying with Fabio. I didn't think to clarify what *you guys* meant. I thought it was all three of you."

Sassy began to cry. My stomach dropped to my toes.

"Bad things happen to those who destroy greatness," Mae Blockinschlokinberg hissed, enjoying the unfolding drama. "Bad voodoo."

"Shut your trap," I snapped at her and scanned the note. "It's Zorro's handwriting. He wrote this."

"What does it say?" Zach asked, looking over my shoulder.

"Says we never should have murdered the Queen," I read aloud, confused.

"Oh my Goddess," Sassy gasped out, covered from head to toe in applesauce. "You guys offed Freddie Mercury?"

"No, we didn't off the greatest singer in the world other than Steve Perry," I said with an eye roll.

"Read the rest," Zach said.

I nodded. My hands trembled. "Willow and Zach, I am leaving Assjacket. I can no longer live with the guilt of killing our Queen. We never should have murdered her. We will pay. I'd suggest you repent as well. Zorro."

"Who is the Queen?" Roger asked, perplexed.

"I don't know a Queen," I said, shaking my head. It was Zorro's handwriting, but not his voice. He rarely got through a sentence without the word guurrlfriend in it. "Do you know a Queen?" I turned to Zach.

Zach's eyes had dilated and his fury made everyone in the room take a step back except me. He was a deadly magical volcano about to erupt. Sadly, I'd seen him like this many times and it broke my heart to see it again. His fingers sparked ominously and the bellow of agony that left his mouth came from deep in his chest. The entire Assjacket Community Center shook on its foundation and more applesauce, along with a dozen boxes of chocolate chip cookies, exploded.

"Talk to me," I begged.

Zach's entire body was filled with rage. His eyes blazed. They were feral and unseeing. I didn't need to ask who the

Queen was anymore. I remembered now. The piece of shit who'd bought him and tried to destroy him had occasionally referred to herself as the Queen. I supposed that I'd tried to block the past out. However, it all came roaring back.

Fabio stepped into the room and put his hand on his son's shoulder. "Who is the Queen, Zach?"

Zach's eyes closed and he growled like an animal. "The Queen is Henrietta Smith. The unholy bitch who bought me and cursed me to a living hell."

"Fuck," Fabio snarled and pivoted around. "They're gone."

"Who's gone?" I asked, my eyes still on Zach.

"Mae Blockinschlokinberg and her nasty little minimes," Bob shouted. "I didn't even see them leave."

"They're slugs," Sassy said, digging through the applesauce frantically just in case they had shifted and hidden. "They probably shifted and slithered out. Too bad applesauce isn't salted. That would have shown them."

"That's why she knew our names," I whispered, putting the horrifying puzzle pieces together. "Mae Blockinschlokinberg came here for revenge."

"I'm sorry, what?" Roger asked, gently putting his hand on Zach to calm him.

"When did that woman and her people decide to come here? Did you seek her out?" I asked.

"We did not," Bob said, shifting back to his human form. "She sent word through a homing pigeon that she was going to grace us with her presence."

"Before or after Zorro was set to do the show?" I demanded.

"After," Bob said, wringing his little hands. "You think they kidnapped Zorro?"

My eyes filled with tears and I nodded. "Or worse." Zorro was the easiest of us to capture, because he was the most trusting. Plus, he fainted when in peril. He was clearly forced to write the note. How he was forced, I could barely bring myself to think about. He'd already been through hell in his life due to the horrifying beatings he'd taken from his pack for being gay and he was right back there now.

"Mac said they were staying in the woods on the outskirts of town," Zach ground out, still on the edge of detonating. "Who knows the woods around Assjacket?"

"I do," Fabio said. "Mac does as well. We can split into groups and find Zorro."

"The trees can help as well. I can speak with them." My level of fear and frustration almost strangled me. I would beat drums and dance naked in front of a whole stadium of man-titties if it meant getting my best friend back from Mae Blockinschlockinberg's evil clutches.

"My chipmunks know the woods too," Sassy volunteered. "They're not killers since they're vegetarians, but my boys can kick some serious ass. I'll call Jeeves and have him take our kids into the forest to search."

"If they find them, tell them to secure Zorro's safety," Zach instructed tightly. "Mae Blockinschlokinberg is mine."

"And mine," I added.

Zach snapped back into reality and his eyes bored into mine. "Willow, this one is on me. It's for all the people who aren't here anymore. If Henrietta Smith has followers as it seems she does, it's my responsibility to end them. I'll like myself a whole hell of a lot if I put an end to this sadistic bullshit."

I nodded. I understood. "Mae Blockinschlokinberg is all yours."

"Thank you," he whispered as he pulled me into his strong arms and kissed me like there would be no tomorrow.

I hoped that wasn't the case, but just in case, I kissed him right back.

"We'll get him back," Zach whispered to me. "We've lost too much already. I promise we won't lose Zorro, too."

I nodded and held onto hope. Zorro had done it for Zach and me, multiple times, and I wouldn't dishonor his friendship by giving up before we started.

"Mac and Zelda are on their way," Fabio said, putting his phone back in his pocket. "Bob and Roger, do you have any personal information on Mae Blockinschlokinberg?"

Roger bounced on his toes and nodded his head. "She filled out paperwork for taxes."

"Excellent," Fabio said. "As long as she didn't forge anything or lie, we can trace her. If she leaves town, we can go after her. Have Simon the skunk hack into the government database and find out everything we can about this ghastly woman."

"Simon hacks?" Sassy asked, surprised and impressed.

"He does. Don't tell Zelda. She'll think I taught him how to do it," Fabio told her.

"Did you?" Sassy asked.

"Yes," Fabio admitted. "But that's neither here nor there. Right now, we have to find some slugs."

"We're here," Zelda said as she and Mac poofed into the applesauce and crumb covered dressing room. "What in the ever-lovin' hell?"

"I crashed into the wall and the applesauce exploded," Sassy said, shaking the excess goop off her broom. "Did you know I was the Postmistress?"

"I think everyone knows except you," Zelda told her as she scanned then sniffed the note I handed her. "Flowers."

"What?" Zach asked, stressed to his limit. "What flowers?"

"The note has a scent," she said, sniffing it again and wincing. "Old lady crouch and flowers. They're near flowers."

"What part of the forest has flowers in bloom right now?" I asked.

"Wait," Zelda said, sniffing the note yet again. "Dang it. I can't quite place the smell."

"Let me try," I said, reaching for the note. "I'm a dryad, and I teach botany. I'm pretty good at the nature stuff."

"You go, Willow! You've got this," Bob said sweetly, echoing my earlier sentiment to him.

Closing my eyes, I raised the note to my nose. "Goddess," I muttered, then gagged. "Old lady crouch is rank."

"You got that right," Zelda agreed. "Can you smell the flowers?"

I nodded slowly and smiled. "Roses. They're near roses."

"I'm the only one with roses in Assjacket," Fabio volunteered.

"Perfect," Mac said, sounding every bit the sheriff of Assjacket combined with the King of the Shifters. "We'll divide up and approach Fabio's house from all sides. Poof in about a mile out and make your way in. I have backup already searching. I'll redirect to the new location."

"On it," Zach said. "Willow and Fabio are with me. We'll come up in front of the house."

"Good call," Zelda said, all business. "Mac and I will take the back side. Willow, how well can you manipulate the trees?"

"Very well," I said. "How about you?"

"All the fucking trees in the world are my minions," she said with an eye roll. "Between the two of us and Mac's unbelievable and seriously sexy affinity with manipulating nature, we should be set if we need the trees."

"What can Mac do?" I asked, curious.

Mac grinned. "Mac can open the earth and send Demons back to Hell."

"Sweet Goddess in a tutu," I said, bowing my head in respect. "Mac's insane."

"With a fine ass to boot," Zelda added, pointing to her mate's nice rear end.

"And my mate Jeeves is a kangaroo Shifter with a *huge* package who kicked the Demons back to hell after Mac with the fine ass opened the earth," Sassy announced with pride.

Mac shook his head and smiled. "I'll have Jeeves gather the chipmunks and come up on the right," Mac said, texting his adopted kangaroo son.

"I'll take care of that and meet up with them," Sassy said, with her blonde applesauce covered hair blowing around her head like a witchy badass. "Oh, and just so no one gets confused, I'll be speaking British during the battle. Make sure no one shouts orders in Canadian or I'll fuck everything up."

"Noted," Mac said, closing his eyes for a brief moment.

"I'm out." Sassy took off on her broom like a bat out of hell.

Fabio turned to Bob and Roger. "Find Simon and have him hack all the information he can find on Mae Blockinschlokinberg. We might need it."

"Simon hacks?" Zelda asked, eyeing her father suspiciously. "Since when?"

"Since Fabio taught him how," Roger volunteered then covered his mouth with both hands. "I don't think I was supposed to say that."

"Umm… nope," Fabio agreed with an apologetic shrug to his daughter. "If it helps, Simon asked. I was simply being cordial and taught him."

Zelda narrowed her eyes. "Is it useful right now?" she asked.

"Very," Mac said with a curt nod. "Also, very illegal. I'm going to pretend I didn't hear any of this conversation. We'll talk about it after we apprehend the slugs."

I still couldn't get over that Mae Blockinschlokinberg and her posse were slug Shifters. On the other hand, it made perfect sense that a slug would have some kind of affiliation with Henrietta Smith. After all, both creatures were bottom-feeding bitches.

"What about the left side of the house?" Zach asked, getting back on topic. "Will that be covered or should we create smaller groups?"

"Shifters," Mac said, texting the instruction out on his phone. "My brother will pull a crew together and take the left."

"Are the cats back?" I asked. They were incredible in battle. Any magic thrown at them bounced right off and flew back at the attacker.

"They're on their way. And I think they found the investor," Zelda said.

"Doesn't matter," Zach told his sister. "Sassy ate the check, so the investor's money is safe."

"I'm not touching that," Zelda muttered.

"Probably smart," I told her. "She offered to poop it back out, but I don't think Mae Blockinschlokinberg was too keen on that."

"Again," Zelda said with a laugh. "Not touching it."

"Ready?" Fabio asked, looking at both of his children with pride. "It's time to salt some slugs."

"Never been more ready in my life," Zach said. "Let's move."

CHAPTER FOURTEEN

THE WOODS SURROUNDING FABIO'S PROPERTY WERE DENSE. A foreboding wind blew and the sky darkened ominously. The trees swayed and groaned. My stomach wasn't happy.

"Is a storm expected?" Zach asked quietly as we made our way through the thick underbrush looking for anything suspicious.

"Wasn't in the forecast," Fabio said, looking up. "However, Sassy is in charge of the forecast, so..."

"Sassy certainly has a lot of jobs," I commented, touching as many tree trunks as possible to see if there was a message for me that might help. I was almost sure my wooden friends had something to say, but I couldn't figure it out.

"We had an Assjacket job fair, and Sassy beat everyone to the sign up," Fabio said, chuckling while thoroughly searching every inch of the forest floor. "I think she thought she was signing up to win something. She threw a shitfit when it was suggested she might want to let the others have a shot. In the end, we decided that the buildings in Assjacket meant more than division of the jobs."

"Sassy blows up buildings?" Zach asked, scanning the area with deadly precision.

"And then some," Fabio replied dryly. "Her mate Jeeves has been an outstanding influence on her, though. He's the nicest man in the Universe. Loves her to a distraction."

"I was under the impression that kangaroo Shifters were extinct," I said.

"Jeeves is the last one," Fabio whispered, motioning for us to get low. "Do you smell that?"

It was faint, but it was there. "Old lady crouch," I whispered, wrinkling my nose. Sniffing the wind, I made a calculation. "About a quarter of a mile straight ahead."

"There's a stream there," Fabio informed us. "Land is marshy and wet. More of a valley than flat ground."

"Sounds right for slugs," Zach muttered as his eyes and hands sparked with barely contained magic.

"Tamp it back, big guy," I said, touching his arm. "If you set the forest on fire, you'll announce we're here. That's bad theatre. We're going for more of a surprise entrance. You feel me?"

Zach nodded and pulled back his power with effort. "I feel you right here," he said, touching his heart.

My smile came automatically. "I feel you right here too," I replied, touching my heart. I also felt him in other places, tingly places, but that conversation could wait until later. Right now, we had to find our BFF.

"Stop it," Fabio said. "You're both going to make me cry.

If I cry, I get blotchy. I want to look my best when squishing slugs."

"You're nuts," Zach said with a grin. "Truly insane."

"And you have my genes, boy," Fabio said, giving Zach a fatherly slap on the back. "Good luck."

"Don't need luck," Zach replied. "I've got my mate and my father with me."

Both Fabio and I were stunned to silence. He'd called me his mate and acknowledged Fabio as his dad. Two things that, up until now, I wasn't sure would ever happen.

Fabio cried first. I was a close second.

"Umm... I meant that in a good way," Zach said, running his hands through his hair and biting back his exasperation.

"Happy tears," I blubbered. "I didn't think you'd recognized our connection."

Zach pulled me close and rested his chin on my head. "I've always known, Willow—from the first moment I saw you. I simply wasn't free to act on it. Being cursed has some massive disadvantages."

"This is one of the best days of my life," Fabio said, sniffling and pulling himself back together. "I mean, I know we have to kill some shit and save Zorro, but to hear the word *father* come out of your mouth was like an orgasm that blew the top of my head off without the sex. I don't even care if my face is blotchy."

"Your way with words is..." Zach said, searching for something to say that wouldn't be insulting.

"Beautiful," I supplied. "Graphically inappropriate and slightly gross, but beautiful."

"Thank you," Fabio said, joining our hug.

"Welcome," I said, kissing his cheek. "But now's not the time. Zorro first, group love-fest later." I pointed up ahead at an oak I didn't recognize, but its rustling leaves were chittering for my attention. "I'm going into the tree. I think it wants to tell me something. And I can slip up to the top and see what's going on. You two stay right here. I'll be quick."

"And careful," Zach added sternly.

I grinned. "The trees are my home. It's my safe place."

Walking into the trunk of the closet and tallest giant oak, I let my body go and my magic consume me.

Being inside of a tree gave me a feeling of wholeness. It was warm and comfortable and smelled like spring and cookies. My body became a blur of golden and bright green sparkles. Gravity had no hold on me in this state, and I vibrated and shifted colors with the heartbeats of the trees.

"Hi, I'm Willow. Do you mind if I enter and take a peek around? My dearest friend is in danger, and I need to borrow you to see what lies up ahead."

"I'm Nancy Lee," the lovely oak replied with a wiggle of pleasure. "I'd be honored and tree-lighted to be of assis-tree-ence, little dryad."

"Thank you, Nancy Lee," I said. "Sponge Bob is my tree father. I'll share your good deed with him."

"Ohhhhhh," Nancy Lee squealed. "Sponge Bob and I go way back to saplings. He is quite a looker, your father. So leafy and green."

I giggled. "Thank you, I think he's beautiful too. Do you, by any chance, have a message for me?

"I'm not sure, but do you have time for a joke?" Nancy Lee asked, sounding hopeful.

Trees and their punny jokes… *"Yes,"* I said. *"But just one."*

Maybe I was wrong about the message. Odd. However, I'd still be able to see the lay of the land and what was happening.

"I rarely get a visit from a dryad," Nancy Lee explained as she rustled happily. *"It's ex-tree-mely exciting! So, would you like a G rated joke, a PG 13 or an X-rated joke?"*

"PG 13 would be fine." Nancy Lee was a wild one.

"What did the oak tree say when she lost her friends on Spring Break?"

"I'm stumped," I told her. I'd heard the joke a million times, but there was no way I was going to hurt her feelings by ruining her punchline. Trees took their jokes very seriously.

"Where my birches at?" Nancy Lee said as her big wooden body rocked with laughter. *"Get it? I replaced bitches with birches. I'm just so silly!"*

"You are silly," I said with a giggle. *"I'd like to go all the way to your highest limbs, if that's okay. Would you give me a branch up?"*

"With pleasure, Willow," Nancy Lee said. *"Do you have a funny joke? It will be easier to shoot you to the top if I'm laughing."*

"Of course," I told her. *"Umm… how about this one, why are Christmas trees so bad at sewing?"*

"Tell me," Nancy Lee squealed, already giggling.

"They keep dropping their needles."

Nancy Lee shook with laughter from her roots all the way to her highest bough. *"Keep going. More! PG 13 please."*

I felt myself being sucked up higher in the tree. Keeping

Nancy Lee in stitches would get me to the tippy top even faster. My fear for Zorro made it hard to joke, but we needed to find him fast before Mae Blockinschlokinberg did anything heinous to him—if she hadn't already. So, if telling Nancy Lee a few zingers would launch me to the highest vantage point in the shortest amount of time so I could locate my BFF, then zingers it was.

"*Ask and you shall receive,*" I promised the oak.

Nancy Lee's laugh was so high pitched, I could feel it in my stomach.

It tickled and made me giggle. "*What did everyone say about the drunk Christmas tree?*"

"*I don't know,*" she said, quaking with anticipation.

"*They said it was lit every night.*"

On a peal of Nancy Lee's uproarious laughter, I shot straight to the top of the tree. Getting my bearings, I let my mind open up so I could see beyond the safety of Nancy Lee.

And what I saw was devastating.

"*No,*" I whispered. "*No, no, no.*"

Zorro was slumped over the edge of a huge black cast iron kettle. His face was obscured, but there was blood-encrusted his blond hair. His pink assless chaps were filthy and torn. My anger made me short of breath. My need to protect my dear friend overwhelmed me.

The minions shoved him the rest of the way inside the cauldron and stacked firewood beneath it as Mae Blockinschlokinberg sipped on a glass of dark red liquid. The bile rose in my throat. Oh Goddess, no. The slug was doing what Henrietta Smith had done to stay young and powerful

—drinking the blood of magicals—the blood of Zorro. Very soon, she would join Henrietta Smith in hell.

Mae Blockinschlokinbitch was about to die.

"What is it, my dear?" Nancy Lee asked concerned.

"My best friend Zorro," I cried out. *"They've put him in a kettle and are getting ready to start the fire. I have to leaf. Now."*

"As you wish," Nancy Lee said and shook her wooden body with such force I was certain Zach and Fabio would be buried in her leaves. *"Take this. It will make you stronger."*

"Take what?" I asked, as I freefell back to her trunk. Was this the message I had been looking for?

"Close your eyes, little one," Nancy Lee instructed kindly. *"It will only hurt for a moment."*

"Hurt?" I asked, confused as I followed her directions and squeezed my eyes shut. A burning sensation shot through my body like a hot knife through butter. *"Holy shit."*

I felt Nancy Lee's magic enter me and mix with my own. My power fought hers until it decided it was a gift—a very powerful gift. As soon as I gave in to the invasion, the pain disappeared.

My head wreath tingled, and I felt breathless and wild. I wasn't exactly sure what Nancy had given me, but there was no time to ask.

"Thank you, Nancy Lee," I said as I burst from her trunk and back to Zach and Fabio.

"You're welcome, Willow. It's fated, my dear. May the forest be with you," she whispered.

"We have to poof," I insisted frantically to Zach and Fabio who were eyeing me strangely. "Now."

Neither man moved an inch.

"What?" I asked.

"You," Zach said with wonder in his voice. "You're glowing. You're ethereal."

"Quite fetching," Fabio agreed. "Like an angel from the Next Adventure. What exactly happened in the tree?"

"Nancy Lee gave me a little power boost," I said sharply. Zorro didn't have time for me to explain more. "While the compliments are flattering, we have to poof. Immediately. Those batshit crazy freaks are about to boil my bestie."

"Fuck," Zach snarled.

"We could poof, but we'd be at a disadvantage if we landed in the stream or popped in with our backs to the slimy monsters," Fabio said. "How fast can you run?"

"Like the wind," I told him.

"As fast as my mate," Zach said. "Can *you* run, old man?"

Fabio grinned. "I can *leaf* your asses in the dust."

"We'll see about that," I challenged, taking off at a sprint that rendered me invisible to the human eye.

The boys were right behind me.

Everything would be okay.

Everything had to be okay.

The alternative was unacceptable.

CHAPTER FIFTEEN

"Stay low," Zach instructed tersely.

We were crouched in the bushes, casing the scene. Mae Blockinschlokinberg had more than just the handful of mini-mes who had attended rehearsals with her. At least twenty slug Shifters wearing black socks and beige sandals scurried around, readying the fire about to be set under the kettle where Zorro was held captive. The excitement at the impending death of an innocent was macabre and all kinds of wrong. Zach's eyes had narrowed to slits. He was reliving his nightmares… except this time he was awake and could possibly end the horror.

"Oh my Goddess," I choked out and pointed to a pile of dead bodies that had been drained of blood and left to rot. "Are they from Assjacket?"

Fabio squinted at the travesty then his chin dropped to his chest. "No, not Assjackians. However, they were someone to others once."

The squatty minions were tucking kindling in between the logs under the cauldron to make the fire easier to start. Zorro's head tipped back when they jostled the pot with their clumsy efforts. His face was streaked with blood and I couldn't tell if he was breathing.

Knots formed in my throat as I forced myself to stay put. Only fools rushed in, and I couldn't be a fool while Zorro's life was on the line. "We have to get over there. We have to stop her."

"This ends today," Zach hissed his agreement.

"Is Zorro alive?" Fabio whispered, worried.

I put my ear to the forest floor and nodded. I could hear my friend's heartbeat. It was weak, but it was there. It gave me hope. "Barely, but yes. Mae Blockinschlokinberg has been drinking his blood."

"Dead bitch walking," Zach growled in a tone that made the hair on the back of my neck stand up.

"I've sent an enchanted ping to the others so they know our location," Fabio said. "There are too many of them, and not enough of us, right now. If we go in now, they'll be able to get to Zorro before we have a chance to stop them. Let's hold off on an attack until everyone has the area surrounded."

"I'm good with that unless they light the fire," Zach said, his eyes glued to Mae Blockinschlokinberg, who greedily gulped more of Zorro's blood from the chalice she gripped with both hands. "When that happens, I move whether we have backup or not."

"What da fuck are youse guys doin'?" a voice whispered from behind us. "Playin' hide and seek?"

Zach and Fabio jerked around in surprise and almost blasted the three furry dummies into their Next Adventure. Quickly, shoving the cats behind me, I raised my hands to stop an unnecessary shitshow. We had enough deadly problems on our hands.

"It's Zelda's cats," I whispered.

Fabio blew out a long slow breath, and Zach clenched his fists at his side. The tension was so explosive, it was like a time bomb set to go off at any second.

"Guys, you really shouldn't sneak up on people who can send you into the Next Adventure," I whispered, turning around and chastising the cats.

"Good advice, sweet cheeks. Weese got nine lives, but I think weese are down to three," Fat Bastard said, peeking through the bushes to see what was going on. "Holy shee-ot. Thems is slug Shifters."

"And they have Zorro," I said. "Those slugs are disciples of Henrietta Smith. They're murderers." I gestured to the heap of dead bodies. "We're getting Zorro back and ending this shit for good."

"Them slimy mother humpers spit venom," Boba Fett informed us with a shudder. "Youse get slimed and youse is a goner."

"Are you fucking serious?" Zach demanded, pressing the bridge of his nose in frustration at the new information.

"Nope, I ain't banging no body named Serious," Boba Fett said, shrugging his furry shoulders then grabbing his tiny balls. "I've been tryin' to bang a sweet little calico named Marta, but she don't seem to be impressed with my Johnson."

Fat Bastard whacked Boba in the back of the head. "Dat's not what he meant, numbnuts," he huffed. "To answer the question, yes. Them slugs is poisonous."

"You're sure?" I asked. Venom spitting mollusks added a new wrinkle to our rescue plan.

"I always tell the truth even when I'm lyin'," Fat Bastard assured me with a wink.

"Mmkay," I said, squinting at him. We didn't have time for games or riddles right now. "What exactly does that mean?"

"Nothin'," Fat Bastard said with a chuckle. "Just like sayin' it. Youse people have a plan?"

"Not exactly," Zach admitted. "The new intel makes going in and ripping off Mae Blockinschlokinberg's head a little trickier."

"I like the way youse think," Jango Fett chimed in. "Hows about we run some interference and youse do the rippin'?"

"As long as youse stay away from the filthy, fuckin' disgusting, mother humpin', shit stinkin' mouths of dem slugs youse should be okay," Fat Bastard advised.

He'd left himself so wide open, but I wasn't about to point out he had a filthy mouth himself. There was no time.

Zelda, Mac, Sassy, Jeeves and four of the strangest looking little guys poofed in behind the cats. The strange looking ones had to be Sassy's adopted chipmunk sons. Chewing gum a mile a minute, they were tiny in stature and wearing matching plaid rompers. All four had sweet smiles and a shock of wiry brown hair that stuck straight up on their heads that marked them as brothers.

"These are my boys," Sassy whispered with pride. "Chad,

Chip, Chunk and Chutney. You won't understand a thing they say, but they won't hurt you. They're vegetarians."

Zach shook his head to clear Sassy's info right out of it and leaned over to his sister. "The slugs spit venom. We have to stay clear of their mouths or we're goners according to your cats. There's also a pile of dead victims. I'm assuming Mae Blockinschlokinberg has drained and drank their blood. No telling how powerful she might be with all the magic she's consumed."

Zelda began to spark.

Zach put his hand on his sister's and calmed his twin. "We can't help the ones who are gone. But we can save Zorro, and we can sure as hell make sure this never happens to anyone else.

My heart pounded as my worry for Zorro increased. Zach took my hand as well. "We'll get him back. I swear it."

I nodded. I wanted more than anything in the world to save my BFF. But I knew Zorro wouldn't want us to rush in at the expense of more lives. "It's the venom I'm concerned about," I said. "I've never heard of poisonous slugs. What happens if they spit on Zorro? Or us? What kind of venom is it?"

Zelda glanced over at Mac.

He swore under his breath. "I've heard of venomous slug Shifters, but in all my years I've never seen proof they actually existed. Fat Bastard, you're positive?" Mac questioned.

"Youse bet," he said with a nod. "Howevers, it's lookin' to me that Willow might have a few new *qua-leaf-ications* that might help save the day. Might be a little *ex-tree-me*, but it's not *es-tree-onage*."

"Of course, my cats speak tree," Zelda muttered.

"Wait. I can do something to end this?" I asked, surprised. Maybe my siren abilities were the answer. "Do you want me to sing and send the slugs into an orgasmic tizzy? Will that make them goo themselves to death?"

"I could think of worse ways to die," Sassy mused.

"Umm... not gonna to touch that," Zelda said with a groan. "But when all this shit is over, I'm touching *everything*."

"Whiles I would find a humpin' slug show very arousing," Fat Bastard said with a waggle of his kitty brows. "Dem broads is immune to their own venom. I was talkin' about the sap."

"Sap?" I asked, confused.

"What sap?" Fabio demanded.

"Look at dat freakass magical glow," Fat Bastard said, pointing at me. "The dryad is full of it."

Zach's eyes narrowed. "Did you just insult my mate?" he demanded.

"Absofuckinlutely not," Fat Bastard replied, putting his little paws in the air. "Youse been in a tree lately named Nancy Lee?"

"I have," I said, still not following.

The crazy cat chuckled. "Dat tree is a hoot," he said. "If that wooden broad was a cat, I'd get jiggy with her in a hot sec."

"Does that pertain to anything relevant in our current situation?" Zelda snapped, glaring at her familiar.

"Umm... no," he admitted. "But Nancy Lee just so happens to have the sappy antidote to slug venom."

"What the heck are the chances of that?" I asked, shocked and freaking relieved.

"Pretty damn good," Fabio mused. "Slug Shifters are tree killers. It makes sense that the trees would create some kind of magical defense."

None of this made sense, I thought, as I tried to process what Fat Bastard meant about my sap.

Jango tapped a claw to the side of his nose and winked. "Dat Fate works in mysterious ways."

"Shit." Fabio shuddered, glancing around in alarm. "Is she here?"

"Is who here?" Zach asked, confused.

"Never mind bout dat," Fat Bastard said. "What's important is dat Willow can sap all youse fuckers and den youse will be immune to the poison for thirty-six minutes."

"That's kind of exact." I flexed my fingers, still unsure of what Fat Bastard expected from me. "Just thirty-six minutes?"

All three cats shrugged. "Dems the instructions weese was told."

"Sap us," Zach insisted before I could ask the cats where they got the *directions*. "They're close to lighting the fire."

I had no clue how to sap everyone, but that wasn't about to stop me. I hoped it didn't hurt like when Nancy Lee had given me a power boost, but it didn't matter. No pain. No gain.

"Okay, I have no clue what I'm doing, but I'm gonna do it anyway," I told my friends. "Close your eyes just in case the sap sprays everywhere, please."

"Crap," Sassy muttered. "I just got the applesauce out of my hair. Sap is gonna be a bitch to remove."

"Hush, my love," Jeeves said, squeezing her hand. "It's far better than dying. Plus, just think of it as syrup."

"Ohhhh," Sassy said with a little shimmy. "Like when I covered you in syrup and licked it off?"

"TMI," Zelda said with an eye roll. "I really don't want to have to remove your mouth. You feel me?"

Sassy giggled and gave her BFF a thumbs up.

"Once we're sapped, I'm going straight for Mae Blockin-schlokinberg," Zach said.

"I'll get Zorro," I said, insistently.

Zach nodded. "Mac and Zelda can help you, then move him to safety."

"Whatever it takes to get him away out of harm's way," I agreed. After, I would join Zach in a Blockinschlokinberg slugfest. Whether he wanted my help or not. My place was by his side.

"I have my broom," Sassy said. "Jeeves and I can fly him out. I'm not sure he would survive poofing out of here in his state."

Zach nodded and Zelda patted Sassy's back.

"Brilliant," Zelda told her.

"It was?" Sassy asked, delighted.

"Totally," I confirmed.

"I'll go with Sassy and Jeeves," Fabio said. "Zorro will need to be healed. My house is a mile from here. We'll take him there."

"Can you place a protection spell around the house?"

Zach asked without looking at his father. His eyes were glued to every move Mae Blockinschlokinberg made.

"Indeed, I can," Fabio said.

"Weese will just mosey on in and kick some slug ass," Fat Bastard said as his cohorts nodded their agreement.

"Andwewilltietheminknotsandremovethierinnardsandshovethemuptheirasses," one of Sassy's sons announced.

"I'm sorry, what did you say?" I asked.

"No one knows," Sassy said, patting her son on the head lovingly. "But trust me, it was violent."

"Excellent," Mac said, moving up next to Zach. "Zelda, you ready to pop some slugs?"

"Hell. To. The. Yes," she said in a steely tone. "Willow, after you sap us—which we will hopefully survive..." Zelda winked and grinned at me. "Can you guide the trees to encircle the area so not even one slug can escape?"

"Will do," I said. "But my battle goal is Zorro's safety first. Period. If Mae Blockinschlokinberg and her posse get away, I don't give a shit as long as we save Zorro. After that, I'm going in as Zach's second. And if it comes down to it, and Mae Blockinschlokinberg escapes, Zach and I will hunt her down till the end of time. We clear on the mission?"

I warmed as Zach's gaze held mine with so much pride and love, I thought I would burst. "You're a badass," he said.

"I'm your badass," I reminded him then glanced around. "Everyone good?"

"Youse bet your soon to be sapped ass we are," Fat Bastard said, giving me a little kitty thumbs up. Zelda and the others nodded.

Fat Bastard clicked his claws. "Oh, forgot to tell youse. The investor is on the way."

"That's fine," I said, mentally thanking the Goddess for small favors. "We can pay him back all his money when this is over. Sassy ate the check so the money is still in the bank."

"And I pooped it out," Sassy announced. "It's in the septic system now. Mae Blockinschlokinberg will never find it."

There was a brief moment of silence.

"Mmkay," I said, blocking the visual of what Sassy had just overshared out of my brain and sized up our small force. "Close your eyes and get ready to be sapped."

"You go girl," Zelda said. "You've got the balls to make it happen."

"Don't need balls," I said with a quick smile at Fabio. "Vajay-jays are far superior."

"Duuuuude, you are my kind of chick," Zelda said with a grin as she closed her eyes.

Channeling Nancy Lee and her lovely giggle, I waved my hands and said a quick prayer to the Goddess to help me sap my friends with protection from the slug venom.

The Goddess heard me.

The tingle started in my toes and shot right to the top of my head—the very same way I'd shot to the top of the tree. A lightly scented spring breeze blew and I felt magic leave my fingertips and float to the ones I adored. I heard the squishy gasps of surprise and slowly opened my eyes.

"Sweet Goddess in a thong," I choked out, trying not to laugh.

It was as if I'd pulled a Zelda with her pancakes.

Everyone—including me—was covered from head to toe in gooey sap.

"At least it smells good," Zelda grumbled.

"Tastes good too," Sassy said, licking her finger.

"Nope," I said, giving her a look. "You can't eat it until we're done. If you eat it, it won't protect you. Got it?"

"Roger that," Sassy said. "But you should bottle and sell this shit. It's awesome! I would slather Jeeves in it any day of the week. We could call it Seduction Sap. That's German for yummy foreplay goo."

"Noted," I said with a wince then glanced over at my beautiful sap covered mate who I wouldn't mind licking from head to toe once this was over. "You ready?"

Zach nodded, his eyes filled with determination. "Born ready. On three we go."

"One," I said.

"Two," Fabio added.

"Three," Zach said as we all shot from the bushes like bats out of hell.

Although, Hell would be too good for Mae Blockinschlokinberg and her mini-mes, but that was where we planned to send them.

CHAPTER SIXTEEN

THE CLOUDS TURNED BLACK AND RUMBLED WITH FURY. THE
sunny afternoon had been replaced with an ominous dark-
ness that made my sticky, sap covered skin crawl.

The fire had been lit and it roared beneath the iron
kettle holding one of the most precious people in my life.
Zorro's body spasmed in agony as the magical fire heated
the iron and brought the water to a quick and steamy boil. I
sprinted like the wind to Zorro and pulled him from the
blistering water. Squatting in front of the cauldron, I held
him in my arms as Sassy, Mac, Jeeves and Zelda beat back
the advancing venomous slugs.

I swallowed the scream that rose in my throat at Zorro's
near-death state and concentrated on what I was supposed
to do. There could be no broken links in the chain. Calling
to the trees was simple and quick. I marveled as they
uprooted and formed an impenetrable barrier around the
camp. The mighty oaks and pines were stunning amidst the

horror happening around them. I bowed in thanks and they bowed right back.

The chipmunks sprinted around, creating havoc with each step they took. Sassy was correct. Her boys were violent—strangely adorable and completely out of control.

"Whatsatreesfavoritedrink?" one of them yelled to me as he slapped a few slugs with their own beige sandals.

I couldn't believe it, but I understood him. "A tree's favorite drink is root beer," I shouted back.

All four chipmunks laughed hysterically and then proceeded to shred every single tent and all the possessions of slugs with their teeth in a matter of seconds. I made a mental note never to piss them off.

Mae Blockinschlokinberg's crazed evil minions chanted and danced around the fire, thinking they could shove all of us into the kettle now. They moved like they had snakes in their pants. Actually, they did. Slugs were some serious gross.

Mae Blockinschlokinberg gulped back Zorro's blood from the chalice like her life depended on it… or what little life she had left. Zach slowly approached her from behind as the cats flanked him ready to defend and attack.

Mac's vicious roar as he shifted into his wolf sent the nasty freaky slug minions skittering around like they were on fire. I quickly moved Zorro to a safer spot—safe being a very relative word at the moment. But at least we were away from the boiling cauldron.

Sassy made setting the slugs on fire a reality. With a shriek that pierced my eardrum, she choked up on her broom and smacked the minions like they were baseballs and she was playing in the World Series. It was insane.

But then again, Sassy *was* insane—fabulously insane.

"Never wear black socks and beige sandals," Sassy hissed as she knocked slug after slug into the roaring fire.

"Willow, let's get Zorro out!" Zelda shouted over the wailing of the smoldering slugs. She reached for a limp Zorro. Mac, still in his wolf form, guarded her and gnashed his huge deadly fangs at any slug who dared to come near. "Sassy. Jeeves. Take Zorro. NOW."

My heart and my burden lightened a little as Sassy and Jeeves hopped on Sassy's broom and zipped over to Zelda.

The red-haired Shifter Wanker carefully handed Zorro over to Jeeves.

"Hold on, kids. It's gonna be a bumpy ride," Sassy shouted as she flew them away. Fabio soared next to them and they disappeared from sight quickly.

It would be an *oversimp-leaf-ication* to say the battle was a breeze, but the main objective had been accomplished in the first three minutes. Zorro was on his way to safety.

We had thirty-three minutes to close the rest of the deal.

"I didn't want that one anyway," Mae Blockinschlokinberg screeched over the screaming of her burning minions. "It's you I want." She pointed at Zach and began to chant a spell.

"No fucking way," I hissed.

Sprinting faster than I ever had, I launched myself at the woman who was trying to curse my mate. I was very aware that Zach wanted the honor of removing her head, but he might not get the chance if she completed the spell.

The cats appeared right next to me. For lumpy little things, they moved dang fast.

"Duck, Willow," Fat Bastard yelled. "Boba and Jango are gonna throw me. I'm gonna land my fat ass in her mouth so she can't talk."

I was sure I'd heard him incorrectly, but I did as I was told. Zelda's cats were some of the fiercest and most vicious fighters I'd ever come across. If they had a plan, it was probably good.

Or gross.

Definitely gross.

I had not misunderstood. Jango Fett and Boba Fett drop kicked Fat Bastard through the air. They certainly had strong hind legs and good aim. Fat Bastard's ample ass was now wedged in Mae Blockinschlokinberg's mouth. Waving my hands, I covered the certifiable feline oddballs in some extra sap. I didn't want to risk Mae Blockinschlokinberg biting Fat Bastards' ass and killing him.

Although, anything thrown at the cats ricocheted back on the attacker. Maybe that was their plan. However, with the large cat's enormous bottom in her mouth, Mae Blockinschlokinberg wasn't physically able to bite anything.

"They're shifting," Zelda shouted, slapping the slimy bugs off of her. "I'm gonna start popping. It's gonna get messy."

Zach grabbed Mae Blockinschlokinberg from behind and put his hands around her squat neck. Fat Bastard extracted his ass from her mouth and plopped down in front of her. Boba Fett and Jango Fett flanked him ready to insert his big bottom right back into her mouth at a moment's notice.

"Are there more of you than just those here?" Zach growled. "How many other abominations like you are out there in the world?"

"Wouldn't you like to know," she burbled and hissed, slime and blood leaking from her lips.

The cats extended their nails and flashed them in her face. The chipmunks raced over wielding a bag of cellphones.

"Nomorethisisitcheckedtheirphonesthatoneistheleader," one of Sassy's boys said.

"What the hell did youse say?" Jango Fett asked.

"Hackedinfabiotaughtustotalloserslotsofpicturesofdead-victimsletskillem." The chipmunk pointed at Mae Blockin-schlokinberg.

"But I thought you were vegetarians," I said.

"Youse understood dat?" Fat Bastard asked, shocked.

I was a little shocked too. "I did. They're all here. No more. Fabio also taught the chipmunks to hack and they found pictures of the dead victims. Mae Blockinschlokin-berg is the leader. The brothers want to kill the slugs," I said as the boys nodded spastically. "Whatever we do, we have to do it fast." Time flies when you're fighting for your life, and our time was almost up.

As if on cue, Zelda yelled, "We have two minutes." She was covered in slug guts as she continued to pop slug after slug.

"Kill me," Mae Blockinschlokinberg snarled. "See if I care. Henrietta Smith, my Queen, will save me."

185

"No one can save you," Zach said coldly. "Sadly, none of the people you killed will be able to enjoy your demise."

"My death is my beginning," Mae Blockinschlokinberg bellowed, turning purple in her rage. "Those whose blood I drank should feel honored by their sacrifice."

"Gonna go out on a limb and say you're wrong," I said.

Mae Blockinschlokinberg glared at me and bared her teeth. "I hear dryad blood is tasty. I will come for you and make you my blood slave along with Zach just like my Queen did. I will destroy you and everything you love—Zorro, your friends and those little babies you're so fond of. Their blood will be delicious. I will own all of you for eternity. All of you lessers will die violently by my hand after I gorge on your blood and become unstoppable. I will tear out your entrails and eat them with a spoon and a nice chianti. I shall rule the world, you lowly pieces of shit."

Fat Bastard rolled his eyes and raised his hand. "Hey Zach, wesse is down to one minute here. If Mae Blockin-schlokinshitforbrains is done monologuin', you should probably get to the head rippin' part. Youse feel me?"

Zach glanced sadly over at the pile of victims and looked up to the sky for guidance from the Goddess. A sliver of sunlight burst through the black clouds and a light sprinkling of sparkling silver rain fell from the sky. The Goddess cried for the ones who could no longer fight for themselves.

"Do you have any last words?" Zach demanded. "Are you sorry for what you have done? Repent now and the Goddess might show you mercy."

"Your Goddess is nothing," Mae Blockinschlokinberg

hissed as spittle dripped down her chin and her eyes were wild. "I am the Goddess."

"Wrong answer," Zach said flatly as he quickly and efficiently ended the vile life of a woman who never should have existed with one incredibly strong head twist. It wasn't bloody. It wasn't loud.

The self-proclaimed slug queen went down with a crazed smile on her face as if she had a secret. She was whack-a-doodle.

And she was gone.

"Ding dong the blood-thirsty bitch is dead," Zelda said, walking over and glancing down emotionlessly at the body of Mae Blockinschlokinberg. "How do you feel?" She looked at Zach.

He shook his head. "I've never ended a life," he said, staring at the woman lying on the ground. "I feel relieved. I don't feel bad and I don't feel good. I did what had to be done to protect the people I love and to avenge those who no longer need anyone's protection."

"Ending someone is never easy—no matter how evil," Mac said, shifting back to human and pulling on some jeans. "Doing the right thing and then having to live with it can be difficult. However, if it's me, or an unhinged lunatic murderer... I prefer me."

"Dat one was batshit cray-cray," Fat Bastard said. "Even the investor said she was."

"The investor?" I asked.

"Yep, she'll be here any minute now," Fat Bastard started, then screeched a yeeeow when he got picked up and thrown with his cronies to safety by a horrified Zelda.

"What the hell?" Zach shouted, grabbing me and the chipmunks. "Run!"

Mac was hot-footing it right on Zelda's heels.

Mae Blockinschlokinberg did have a secret. A horrible secret.

Mae Blockinschlokinberg wasn't dead. Or not in any conventional way.

A dank wind blew through the forest as the body of Mae Blockinschlokinberg morphed into slugs. Thousands of slugs. Thousands of hissing, spitting, glowing red-eyed, deadly slugs who had one mission...

To kill us.

The Queen might have the final say after all.

CHAPTER SEVENTEEN

"Magic. Use magic," Zelda yelled as we got to the tree line. "Pop them."

Zelda and Zach shot fireball after fireball as the slugs advanced moving faster than I'd ever seen a slug move. Mae Blockinschlokinberg was the freaking Hydra of slugs. All the magical blood she'd ingested was paying off and making our chances of survival look slim. For every slug popped, ten more took their place. There had to be at least three thousand now.

"Trees," I shouted, waving my hands in the air frantically. "Uproot. Step on the slugs."

The giant oaks and pines heeded my command. The sound of the massive trees running toward the slugs rivaled an earthquake combined with a tornado and a tsunami. The chipmunks were terrified. With a clap of my hands, I poofed them to Fabio's house. While they were violent, they weren't killers. Vegetarians didn't like death.

"I can't hold them back," Zelda hissed. "They're going to invade Assjacket."

"Stay behind us," Fat Bastard bellowed. "If them slugs spit, let us take it. We'll send it back and poison them slimy sacks of shit."

"Too many and they're immune to their own poison," Zach yelled, continuing to pop slugs with fireballs. "Also, this is a bad fucking plan we have going here. They're multiplying. We have to find another way to get rid of them."

"Agreed," I said as I watched the trees stomp as many advancing slugs as they could.

"Should we make a run for it?" Zelda asked, still zapping away. "At least we can warn people."

"We can't let them reach town," Mac said, squatting down and connecting with the earth. "I'm going to try to open a crater. Willow, tell the trees to back off."

"The slugs are everywhere," Zach said. "Not sure that's going to work."

"What we're doing now isn't working," Zelda pointed out. "May as well try something else."

"Trees," I called out. "Back away. Return to your home."

Leaves and pine needles rustled and fell to the ground covering the slugs and slowing their advance. Thousands of the little bastards began to eat the leaves.

"Look at that," Zelda said. "Make it happen again, Willow. The leaves are confusing the slugs. They think it's dinner time."

She was right, and I knew exactly how to make a tree shed some leaves. "What was wrong with the tree's car?" I yelled.

The trees paused their retreat and leaned toward me.

"It wooden go!" I told them.

They shook with laughter and their falling leaves covered more of the venomous slugs.

It wasn't destroying them, but it had slowed them down. "How does a tree get on the internet?"

The trees jiggled with excited anticipation.

"They log on," I shouted.

Again, they rocked with laughter.

Again, their leaves fell.

Again, the slugs slowed.

"Another," Zach said.

"On it," I told him. "How did the elm tree know the fig tree wasn't looking for anything serious? It asked for no twigs attached."

It was spring, but it looked like a fall day as massive amounts of leaves floated through the air and landed the ground.

"Should I sing?" I asked, not knowing what else to do. Eating would only distract them for so long, and we still didn't know how to destroy them.

"Not sure thousands of humping slugs is a good thing," Zelda said, shaking her head. "But since I don't have a better idea, go for it. My magic is making it worse."

"As is mine," Zach agreed, snapping his fingers and producing earplugs for all. "Put these in unless you think all of us getting horny is a good plan."

"Not a good plan," Mac said, grabbing a set from Zach and shoving them in his ears. "I like you, but not that much."

"Incoming," Fat Bastard announced at the top of his kitty lungs.

"What the hell?" Zelda grunted as we all got knocked to the ground by a vicious wall of wind.

"Today is going seriously shitty," I muttered, crawling over to Zach and holding onto him, so I didn't blow away.

"I love you," he said. "I love you completely."

Even though we were probably going to die shortly, I smiled from ear to ear. "Do you love yourself?"

"I do—at least I think I do," he said as the wind grew stronger and his smile grew wider. "I love that we were able to save Zorro. I love that I have a family. I'm proud to have avenged those who died at the hand of Henrietta Smith even though it seems to have ended in a deadly slug infestation. I finally believe that I deserve Fabio and Zelda. I believe I deserve you because I'm a good guy. I want to spend the rest of my life making you happy the way you make me happy."

"That's adorable, Brother, but the rest of your lives might only be about five minutes if we don't come up with a new plan," Zelda yelled over the roar of the wind.

"I don't care," I said, hugging Zach hard. "I love you and no matter how much time we have together, it's perfect. I will love you in this life and in the Next Adventure."

"Would someone like to tell me what in the Goddess's gauchos is going on here?" a gorgeous woman demanded as she appeared in a blast of shimmering light.

"Oh fuckballs," Zelda muttered under her breath. "I didn't think this day could get worse."

"Apparently, it can," Mac added.

Even though it was dark and cloudy, the woman's radiance was almost blinding. I had to shield my eyes from the glare.

She was stunning in an otherworldly way and seemed somewhat off her rocker. She stood at least six feet tall and had a figure that belonged to a Barbie doll, perky big boobs and a teeny tiny waist. Clad in army fatigues and combat boots, her attire didn't match her femininity. Tons of thick, curly, rainbow-colored hair framed her breathtaking face. With beautiful black skin and sparkling silver eyes, she was unlike any other being I'd come across in the Universe.

I had no clue who she was, but she seemed to know who we were.

"Get up off the ground," she commanded in a frightening tone.

She snapped her fingers and the winds halted. Glancing around, she wrinkled her nose in disgust when she saw the slugs. Holy crap, this woman might not be aware of the poisonous venom. She definitely seemed dangerous but dying for being scary seemed a little harsh.

Hopping to my feet, I dashed over and yanked her to relative safety.

"May I ask what you're doing?" she demanded as her silver eyes narrowed dangerously and I heard Zelda choke on her own spit.

"Sorry," I said nervously. "It's just that you were kind of close to the slugs and they spit venom. I… umm… didn't want you to die." My voice trailed off as the woman's eyes began to shoot sparks.

"Excuse me for a moment," she said as she walked about

twenty feet away then threw a fit like I'd never witnessed in my life.

The woman spewed out some rather vile profanities and was now dancing around like she had a colony of fire ants in her pants—branches were falling and rocks were flying. Ducking, I grabbed Zelda with a look of terror in my eyes. Zach and Mac immediately huddled with us. However, the cats watched and laughed like felines with a death wish. The woman was insane and so were the cats.

"Who is that?" I asked Zelda.

"Fate."

"Oh my Goddess," I choked out. "I just pissed off Fate?"

"Possibly," Zelda said with a shudder. "But I think that's her being happy."

"That's happy?" I asked, shocked. "She's like a shitstorm on steroids."

"You got that right," Zelda agreed. "You definitely don't want to see her when she's mad."

"How do we stop this? That crazy freak is going to level Assjacket and kill all of us if she keeps going," I hissed. I couldn't believe the slug infestation was now the least of our worries where the town was concerned.

"Not a clue," she said. "Normally, Fate just has to work it out. Although, she's gonna cause an avalanche at the rate she's gyrating."

Since I was probably going to die today anyway, I had nothing to lose. This was ridiculous. At least the slugs had paused their attack to watch Fate unravel.

"Okay, that's enough," I shouted over the noise. "You will stop behaving like a whack job on crack right now."

"Or *what?*" Fate demanded, pausing to see what I was going to do.

"Umm… or nothing," I said, exasperated. "It's been a really bad day, and we're probably about to bite it. So, this just isn't working for me."

"Okay," Fate said, striding back over like nothing was out of the ordinary.

"I can't fucking believe that worked," Zelda whispered.

"Neither can I," I whispered back.

"Who are you?" Zach demanded, eyeing the woman.

"It's Fate," Mac said with a curt nod of respect to the nutjob in question. "To what do we owe the pleasure?"

"He meant displeasure," Zelda chimed in.

"Ahhh, if it's not the soon to be Baba Yaga," Fate said, eyeing Zelda with a smirk.

"And if it's not the winner of the Toddler Tantrum of the Universe," Zelda shot back. "Why are you here? And PS, we don't have much time. Kind of trying to figure out how to off the slugs and live to see tomorrow."

"I came to see my investment," Fate said coolly, crossing her arms over her chest and stomping her foot. "Wanna see where my money went."

"You're the investor?" Zach asked, confused. "You're the one who put two hundred thousand into the Assjacket Community Theatre?"

"Yep," she said as the cats waddled over and sat at her feet. "I just loved the musical version of *The Silence of the Lambs*. Sooooo realistic. I want to see my show or I'm going to throw a fit."

195

"Like the one you just threw?" Zach asked as neutrally as he could.

"That was not a fit," Fate said. "That was a warmup."

"Your money is in the bank," I told her quickly, keeping my eye on the deadly slugs who were done with their snack and on the move again. "Sassy ate the check and... well, never mind. Suffice it to say we can pay you back every cent."

"Don't want my money back," Fate said, looking like she was on the verge of leveling the state of West Virginia. "I want to see a show."

"Now?" I asked.

"Right now," she replied.

I turned to Zach with wide eyes. He shrugged and then went for it. "It's *Jaws—the musical*," he explained. "Mac is the umm... shark."

"That's right," Mac said, wildly confused.

Zach blew out a relieved sigh that Mac had played along. "Normally, Mac would wear pink assless leather chaps, but since we're not at the theatre we'll have to go without costumes."

"Thank the Goddess for that," Mac said.

"No worries," Fate said with a wicked little grin. She wiggled her fingers and Mac's ass was now on display for the world in pink leather assless chaps.

Zelda slapped her hands over her mouth and tried not to laugh. She failed. I laughed, too, but swallowed it when I noticed the slugs were getting dangerously close.

Crap.

"I'm the sheriff. I'll be playing the role as a man," I said quickly. "Zach is the marine biologist played as a woman, and Zelda is the captain. She'll be performing the captain as a hermaphrodite."

"Are you serious?" Zelda shouted, appalled.

"Completely," I hissed, nodding my head toward the advancing slugs.

Fate clapped her hands. I was now in a sheriff's uniform. Zach was in a lab coat and a speedo and Zelda was wearing a potato sack and weathered yacht cap. I was unsure how a potato sack represented a hermaphrodite sea captain, but I wasn't about to ask.

"What about the set?" Fate asked.

"What do you mean?" I asked, getting frantic.

"Doesn't *Jaws* take place on a lake in a boat?" Fate inquired as the cats started to chuckle.

Mac was going to die in pink leather assless chaps. I was going to die looking like Roy Scheider. Zach was going to bite it in a speedo. And Zelda was going to the Next Adventure in a sack that held carbs.

"Actually," I said. "*Jaws* doesn't take place on a lake. It takes place..." I gasped and almost passed out.

Zach steadied me while inching the group away from impending death. If the slugs didn't kill us, Fate might.

Fate watched me closely and with great interest. Her brows were raised, and a small smile pulled at her lips.

"Will you create the set I ask for?" I inquired as Sassy's and Fabio's comments from earlier bounced in my head and smacked me in the brain.

"Ready?" Fabio asked, looking at both of his children with pride. "It's time to salt some slugs."

"They're slugs," Sassy said, digging through the applesauce frantically just in case they had shifted and hidden. "They probably shifted and slithered out. Too bad applesauce isn't salted. That would have shown them."

Fate's smile was positively wicked. "Depends on what you ask for."

My mind raced. Could it be that simple? I mean, it would be seriously gross... but so very simple. It could also wash away Assjacket, but I somehow didn't think that was Fate's plan.

"Do you see the future?" I demanded.

"I might," Fate replied cryptically.

"Do you control it?" I pressed as Zach, Mac and Zelda watched the exchange with confusion.

"Nope," she said, enjoying the game. "I only see it. I don't decide it. You do, dryad."

Bingo.

"Jaws the Musical takes place on the ocean. A SALT-WATER ocean," I yelled.

"As you wish," Fate said with a cackle.

"Brilliant," Zach yelled. "How did we not think of that?"

"Shit," Zelda yelled. "We're idiots."

"Almost dead idiots," Mac added.

"Almost but not quite," Fat Bastard shouted. "I didn't think youse dumbasses would ever come up with it."

"You knew?" Zelda snapped at her cats.

"Hell to the no," Fat Bastard said with an eye roll. "Youse think I would have embedded my fine ass in dat woman's smelly mouth if I knew how to off her? I meant that when

198

dis hot piece of woman called Fate is involved, everything usually turns out fine."

Fate winked at Fat Bastard and snapped her fingers. A saltwater ocean gushed into the valley.

"We're going to need a bigger boat. Or at least a hole to put the ocean in," Mac said with a whistle. He dropped to his knees and opened the earth. It filled with the salty water along with the screaming and disintegrated slugs. It was a symphony to my ears.

The dark clouds disappeared, and the sun shone brightly. The Goddess was pleased.

And Mae Blockinschlokinberg would never harm anyone again.

Calling back the trees, I silently asked for a border so the ocean didn't flow into Assjacket. They obeyed without question and giggled the entire time.

"We're going to live," Zach shouted joyously, grabbing me and kissing me senseless.

"And I'm not going to bite it in a butt-ass ugly sack and a shitty captain's hat," Zelda sang, dancing around as the slugs withered away shrieking in agony.

"Yet somehow, I'm still wearing pink leather assless chaps," Mac pointed out, shaking his head.

"And I'm still waiting for my show," Fate informed us.

She clapped her hands. A chair, a supersized box of popcorn and a bottle of bourbon appeared. She sat down, crossed her long legs and raised a brow.

"Are you serious?" Zelda demanded with an eye roll.

"Completely," she said. "Start acting, witch."

"If Sassy was here, she'd wax your sorry ass," Zelda grumbled.

"What was that?" Fate asked in a tone that made everyone run to get into places for a show we'd never rehearsed with a cast who wasn't even in the show.

Zelda wasn't a dummy. "I said if Sassy was here, she'd umm… tax your safari gas."

Or maybe she was a dummy.

Fate tapped her toe and checked her diamond-studded watch. "I'm waiting."

"On three?" Zach suggested with a pained expression that made me giggle.

"What the hell are we supposed to do?" Mac asked, bewildered.

"Wing it," Zelda told him. "We've all seen *Jaws*, right?"

Everyone nodded and started laughing.

"One," Zelda said.

"Two," I chimed in.

Zach was still laughing. It was beautiful. He was finally free. Well, after the performance, he would be.

"Three," he said.

And we gave Fate her show.

It sucked. The cats booed us, and Zelda zapped the shit out of them. Mac made up a song about needing a bigger boat, and Zach and I grunted like kidneys and bowels. Sadly, Zorro wasn't here to pole dance and Sassy couldn't sing in German, but in the end, it was… awful. Awful and awfully beautiful.

Thankfully, Fate felt like she'd gotten her money's worth

and decided to let the Assjacket Community Theatre keep her investment for the next show.

As the crazy immortal woman stood to leave, I marched right over to her and threw my arms around her. If she had another tantrum, so be it. I heard Zach gasp and Zelda squeak in horror. Mac groaned and the cats backed away. I didn't care. My guess was that not too many people showed Fate any affection—and with good reason. She was really scary.

"Thank you," I whispered. "You saved us."

"You're wrong," she said, patting my back awkwardly. "I don't create destiny, child. I just know it."

"We wouldn't have figured it out," I insisted, hugging the dangerous woman tighter. "Without you, we'd be goners and so would all of Assjacket. You're wonderful."

"That's a given," she said, extracting herself from my hold and eyeing me with amusement. "I'm fabulous."

I nodded and laughed.

"And since I'm so freaking amazing," Fate said with a grin that made me uncomfortable. "I'm putting in a request."

"For?" I asked, terrified.

"The next Assjacket Community Theatre show," she replied silkily.

"Shit," I heard Zach mutter.

"Fuck," Zelda added.

"*Shaun of the Dead* told through interpretive dance," Fate announced much to everyone's semi-delighted surprise.

"I love that movie," Zach said with a grin.

"Lots of opportunities for the audience to get mamboed by zombies," Zelda pointed out with a wince.

"Makes it exciting," Fate insisted. "Interactive cannibalistic theatre is invigorating."

"Says the freak that won't have to heal all the Shifters who lose their limbs," Zelda said.

Fate slapped her hands on her hips and prepared to throw a fit. "Do we have a deal?"

Looking at my beaten and battered friends, I shrugged and smiled. Zach winked. Zelda rolled her eyes and Mac gave me a hesitant thumbs up.

"Yes, Fate. We have a deal."

Fate grinned and disappeared on the Winds of Change. Five seconds after she vanished, an exhausted Fabio poofed back.

"Zorro's good," he said, looking around at the carnage and the new ocean on his property. "He's still weak, but he's going to be all right."

My hand went to my mouth as a sharp sob of *re-leaf* left my lips. The news was beautiful.

Zach took my hand in his and pulled me close. He inhaled deeply and looked at everyone. "Thank you. All of you. I don't have the words to explain myself, so thank you will have to suffice. Zorro and Willow have been my family —my entire world for a long time… and now our trio has expanded."

I smiled my encouragement and squeezed his hand.

"I have a sister," he said with a nod to Zelda then turned to Fabio. "I have a father and I have friends."

"Dude, you fell in love with yourself waaaay faster than I did," Zelda said, giving her brother a quick hug.

"Getting there," he said. "I also have a mate that I would die for, but who I also want to live for."

My heart skipped a happy beat. I knew I was glowing and that my head wreath was on blossom overload. "Back at you," I told the love of my life.

Zach loved himself. He was finally free to love me, wholly and completely. I kissed him until my entire body buzzed with pleasure. I looked around at our smiling family and friends and blushed. "And I can't wait for us to start living... umm, a little more privately."

EPILOGUE

My heart raced and my body tingled from head to toe.
I struggled to catch my breath and couldn't believe I hadn't
died of pleasure in the last three hours of aerobic sexual
activity.

Zach was a freaking machine.

"Goddess," Zach said, running his hands through his hair
and smiling with smug male pride. "Was that as good for
you as it was for me?"

"Better," I said, cuddling up to him and running my
hands hungrily over his muscular chest, wondering if he
could do it again.

I mean, fourteen orgasms in three hours was pretty dang
impressive, but as exhausted as I was, I wanted more. I
would never get enough of my warlock.

"I love you, dryad," he whispered, playing with my hair
and pulling my very satisfied naked body closer.

"The feeling is mutual, warlock," I replied.

Two weeks had passed since the slugfest, Zorro was back to his awesome self, the new musical had gone off with an insane bout of hilarious hitches, and I was in the arms of the man I loved. Plus, we'd finally gotten some of that privacy I'd been craving. Zelda and Mac had loaned us their Floating Nookie Hut for as long as we wanted it. The Floating Nookie Hut was a treehouse that Mac had built for Zelda to make up for her never having had a treehouse as a child. It was situated in a magical meadow surrounded by glorious trees and riotous beds of wildflowers. The lovely interior was one large open room dominated by a massive king-sized bed. It was light and airy and positively perfect.

We'd been holed up in the hut for three days and counting. I didn't see us leaving for another few weeks.

"I can't believe it's over," Zach said, tracing my lips with his finger.

"I can't believe no one died," I added with a giggle. "Did you see the look on Bob's face when Sassy tried to eat his arm?"

Zach chuckled. "Sassy takes her acting very seriously," he said dryly. "She claims she was performing in Canadian."

"Thought she didn't understand a word of Canadian."

"My point exactly," Zach said. "We're lucky we have three healers in town. Zelda needed Fabio and me on this disaster. She would have been passed out for a month if she'd had to heal all the bites, bruises, amputations and head wounds on her own."

"It was a dreadful choice of a show," I said, laughing as I remembered Roger warbling a barely passable rap song about zombies gnawing on femurs. Half the audience left at that point, but Fate was delighted and that was pretty much all that mattered. She was the investor, after all.

Zorro had played Shaun in the interpretive dance version of *Shaun of the Dead*. Since he'd missed out on the debacle known as *Jaws*, he'd recycled his pink leather assless chaps and wore them with pride while hunting zombies, that was, of course, when he wasn't displaying his prowess on the pole.

Bob had not only written the show, he directed it as well. Roger had composed the appallingly awful songs and did the choreography. It was outstanding that both of the men had day jobs. Their futures were not in the arts. But as Fabio had said, passion that outweighs talent can be beautiful. Fabio was correct. Sassy played most of the other characters and spoke in a *different* language for each one. It was mind-blowing and all kinds of wrong. It kept the audience scratching their heads in confusion the entire *six* hours of the show.

Thankfully, Zach and I had opted or rather begged to work on the stage crew. I was done with my acting career after getting booed by the cats as the sheriff in *Jaws*. Zelda flat out refused to be in the show but did agree to stand by as the magical medic.

That was necessary. It was a hot bloody mess.

Although, having the Tennessee Man-Titty Thespians show up for the opening night performance and leave positively pea green with envy made the entire shitshow worth it—even the gory parts. Bob was still on a high that would last a long time.

Zach kissed my neck and I wiggled with excitement. It

207

was *enormously* clear that my warlock was ready to *go* again. I had very *hard* evidence pressed against my thigh.

"We kicked ass in couples therapy," Zach said as his mouth moved from my neck a little bit lower.

"Yep," I agreed, arching my back. "We were a one and done."

"It felt great to hear Roger confirm my *be-leaf* that I'd learned to love myself," Zach said, looking up at me. "Although, I didn't need him to tell me. I figured it out myself."

"You're very lovable," I told him. "And quite sexy when you're talking Puntreelish."

"Thank you," he said. "You're *ex-tree-mely* lovable and sexy yourself."

"Although, we should have pretended we had a few more issues. Maybe we wouldn't have had to listen to Roger sing a medley of cannibalistic tunes from the show for the rest of the hour," I pointed out with a wince.

"True," Zach said with a laugh. "It was very…"

"Graphic," I supplied. "Unappetizing and horrifying. I couldn't eat for two days after that session."

"Thank the Goddess we don't have to hear anymore," Zach said, pulling my very willing body on top of his. "I spoke with Sponge Bob."

"You did?" I asked, surprised. Only dryads could speak to trees. Well, Zelda could, but they were her minions. "How?"

"It seems that when a warlock wants to mate with a dryad, her tree pappy sends a bit of magic his way," he explained.

"Interesting," I said, intrigued. "What did you talk about?"

"Well, after politely listening to tree puns for an hour and swearing I'd become fluent in Puntreelish, I asked his permission to make you my mate. Officially."

Again, my heart raced. It was all so romantic. My parents were no longer on this plane. They wouldn't ever be able to meet the love of my life. But I had a surrogate father who adored me. The thought that Zach respected my relationship with Sponge Bob made me love him even more.

Assjacket had accepted us just like Zach's family had. And just like my family, Sponge Bob and the boys, had accepted Zach. We even made a plan to make Assjacket our home. My warlock was going into the healing business with his sister, and I was going to teach botany at the new Assjacket elementary school. And Zorro had plans to introduce the Assjackians to the magic of pole dancing and fainting goat yoga at the community center. Never in my wildest dreams did I think I would put down roots in such an enchanted place.

"And what did my tree pappy say?" I asked.

"He said that whatever made his little dryad happy made him *tree-lighted* as well," Zach shared. "He then told me to make like a tree and *leaf* to go find his little dryad and begin our journey together."

"He's a good father," I said with a happy sigh. "And speaking of good fathers…"

"Yep," Zach admitted with a grin. "Fabio wins the category, too, along with being the most honest criminal and best pancake maker in the Universe. I almost called him dad the other day, but we were in public, and I know how he hates to get blotchy."

"I'm pretty sure he'd be fine with getting hives over that one," I told Zach. "Baba Yaga is something else."

Baba Yaga and Marge had arrived back in Assjacket shortly after the slugs were gone for good. Madonna had taken a restraining order out on both of them. They were quite put out with the development. Zelda had gleefully pointed out that if they disobeyed the order, they'd land their asses in the pokey. Baba Yaga didn't think she looked good in orange, so she decided that she liked A Flock of Seagulls better than Madonna anyway.

"I agree. Baba Yaga is a handful," Zach said with a small shudder. "But Fabio adores her. And..." He grinned like a little boy.

"And what?" I asked, grinning, too, even though I had no clue why.

"And they're moving."

My smile turned to a frown. "Why are you happy your dad is moving? You're still getting to know each other."

"Not out of Assjacket," Zach quickly said. "To a new house. Baba Yaga wants something a little more 80s. Lots of shag carpet, mirrored ceilings, built-in lava lamps and disco balls in every room."

I wrinkled my nose and laughed. "Oh my Goddess, that's horrifying."

"Understatement," Zach agreed with a grin. "But Fabio is all for it."

"Still don't understand why you're smiling," I told him, admiring his beautiful face and kissable lips.

"Because Zelda and Fabio want Aunt Hildy's house to stay in the family. Meaning…"

"Meaning they want you to have it?" I shouted, thrilled. I adored the house. It was filled with magic and love.

"Us," he corrected me. "They want *us* to have it. From your reaction, I'm gonna guess that you like the idea?"

"Love," I said dreamily. "I love the idea. What about Zorro?"

Zach smiled. "Not to worry. Mac is building a guest house on their property for Zorro. He's overjoyed. The interior is being done in pink leather."

I winced and grinned at the same time. "All of it?"

"All of it," Zach confirmed.

I sighed and laid my head on my mate's chest. Life couldn't have turned out more perfectly. Well, maybe it could…

"You know," I said, peeking up at my warlock through my lashes. I was aware I was blushing. I could feel the heat on my cheeks. "There are a lot of spare bedrooms in your… *our* new house."

"Your point?" Zach asked, raising a brow and grinning.

"I just thought… you know…" I stuttered, feeling a bit over my head.

Zach kissed my lips hard and rolled me to my back. "I do believe I have the same idea," he said, looking down at me with love and lust in his eyes.

"What's your idea?" I whispered.

"I'd love to fill those rooms with little dryads who look just like you," he said.

"And baby warlocks who look just like you," I added as my need for him increased so much I felt dizzy.

Slowly leaning into me, Zach pressed his lips to my neck. "Would you like to get started on that assignment, Miss Teacher of Botany at the Assjacket School?"

"I would *love* to get started on that assignment, Mister Healer Warlock Partner to the Shifter Wanker," I said, wrapping my arms around him like I would never let go. "Now," I added urgently.

"Your wish is my command, Willow. Always."

My warlock was true to his word. Ten times true to his word. My guess was that we would be adding to our new family unit in the next nine months or so.

And I couldn't be more *tree-lighted*. Life had turned out *tree-mendously*. Not exactly *tree-ditional*, but we were not normal in the human sense of the word. My warlock had all of the *qua-leaf-ications* I'd dreamed about. He was perfect for me.

And I will *guaran-tree* that we will have our happily ever after. Because I will never stop *be-leafing* in my lover, and I know he will never stop *be-leafing* in me.

The End… for now

ROBYN'S BOOK LIST
(IN CORRECT READING ORDER)

HOT DAMNED SERIES
Fashionably Dead
Fashionably Dead Down Under
Hell on Heels
Fashionably Dead in Diapers
A Fashionably Dead Christmas
Fashionably Hotter Than Hell
Fashionably Dead and Wed
Fashionably Fanged
Fashionably Flawed
A Fashionably Dead Diary
Fashionably Forever After
Fashionably Fabulous
A Fashionable Fiasco
Fashionably Fooled
Fashionably Dead and Loving It

GOOD TO THE LAST DEATH SERIES
It's a Wonderful Midlife Crisis
Whose Midlife Crisis Is It Anyway?
A Most Excellent Midlife Crisis
My Midlife Crisis, My Rules

SHIFT HAPPENS SERIES
Ready to Were
Some Were in Time
No Were To Run
Were Me Out
Were We Belong

MAGIC AND MAYHEM SERIES
Switching Hour
Witch Glitch
A Witch in Time
Magically Delicious
A Tale of Two Witches
Three's A Charm
Switching Witches
You're Broom or Mine?
The Bad Boys of Assjacket

SEA SHENANIGANS SERIES
Tallulah's Temptation
Ariel's Antics
Misty's Mayhem
Petunia's Pandemonium
Jingle Me Balls

A WYLDE PARANORMAL SERIES
Beauty Loves the Beast

HANDCUFFS AND HAPPILY EVER AFTERS SERIES
How Hard Can it Be?
Size Matters
Cop a Feel

If after reading all the above you are still wanting more adventure and zany fun, read *Pirate Dave and His Randy Adventures*, the romance novel budding novelist Rena helped wicked Evangeline write in *How Hard Can It Be?*

Warning: Pirate Dave Contains Romance Satire, Spoofing, and Pirates with Two Pork Swords.

NOTE FROM THE AUTHOR

If you enjoyed reading *Your Broom or Mine?*, please consider leaving a positive review or rating on the site where you purchased it. Reader reviews help my books continue to be valued by resellers and help new readers make decisions about reading them.

You are the reason I write these stories and I sincerely appreciate each of you!

Many thanks for your support,
~ Robyn Peterman

Want to hear about my new releases?
Visit robynpeterman.com and join my mailing list!

ABOUT ROBYN PETERMAN

Robyn Peterman writes because the people inside her head won't leave her alone until she gives them life on paper. Her addictions include laughing really hard with friends, shoes (the expensive kind), Target, Coke (the drink not the drug LOL) with extra ice in a Yeti cup, bejeweled reading glasses, her kids, her super-hot hubby and collecting stray animals.

A former professional actress with Broadway, film and T.V. credits, she now lives in the South with her family and too many animals to count.

Writing gives her peace and makes her whole, plus having a job where she can work in sweatpants works really well for her.

Printed in Great Britain
by Amazon

46547173R00139